## Some dreams couldn't touch reality.

He put his hand under her chin, aware of the weight of that dangling cuff. He tilted her head back so that he could plunder her mouth, so that he could taste her.

Hell, in that moment, he wanted to consume her.

His body ached for her. Need pulsed through his veins, and if they weren't in some pit of hell, if the bad guys weren't just down the hallway...

Drew lifted his head. "Then you'd be mine," he rasped.

Tina blinked and shook her head. "What?"

He kissed her once more, just because he had to do it. *There's no way we're dying.* The woman was full of secrets, and he'd be sure he had the chance to discover every single one.

# UNDERCOVER CAPTOR

---

**New York Times Bestselling Author**
## CYNTHIA EDEN

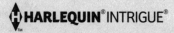

This book is for all of the fantastic Harlequin
Intrigue readers out there—thanks for loving
mystery and romance!

Recycling programs
for this product may
not exist in your area.

ISBN-13: 978-0-373-69741-0

UNDERCOVER CAPTOR

Copyright © 2014 by Cindy Roussos

Printed in U.S.A.

## ABOUT THE AUTHOR

*New York Times* and *USA TODAY* bestselling author Cynthia Eden writes tales of romantic suspense and paranormal romance. Her books have received starred reviews from *Publishers Weekly,* and she has received a RITA® Award nomination for best romantic suspense novel. Cynthia lives in the Deep South, loves horror movies and has an addiction to chocolate. More information about Cynthia may be found on her website, www.cynthiaeden.com, or you can follow her on Twitter (www.twitter.com/cynthiaeden).

## Books by Cynthia Eden

HARLEQUIN INTRIGUE
1398—ALPHA ONE*
1404—GUARDIAN RANGER*
1437—SHARPSHOOTER*
1445—GLITTER AND GUNFIRE*
1474—UNDERCOVER CAPTOR**

*Shadow Agents
**Shadow Agents: Guts and Glory

# CAST OF CHARACTERS

*Dr. Tina Jamison*—Tina's job is to patch up the wounded EOD (Elite Operations Division) agents. She heals them, then sends them back out on new missions. Tina was never supposed to find herself actually *in* the middle of a mission. But a case of mistaken identity has put her in the sights of a terrorist group, and if Tina is going to survive, she will have to put all of her trust in the hands of one dangerous agent.

*Drew Lancaster*—Deadly and controlled, former Delta Force operative Drew Lancaster knows how to survive in any situation. He's currently working undercover for the EOD, and he's ready to risk his life in order to get the job done. But he is *not* ready to risk the life of sexy Dr. Tina Jamison....

*Bruce Mercer*—The director of the EOD is used to standing behind the scenes and pulling the strings as his operatives follow his orders. But when Tina becomes a target—because of *his* secrets—Mercer realizes that it might take more power than even he possesses to save her life.

*Dylan Foxx*—As the leader of an elite group of EOD agents, Dylan's job is to protect his team at all costs. He knows the risks the latest mission poses, and he is more than ready to face the threat coming his way.

*Rachel Mancini*—Darkness has stalked the former marine for years. She understands exactly how it feels to be in the crosshairs of a killer, and Rachel vows to help Tina escape the danger that threatens her.

*Anton Devast*—The desire for vengeance has fueled Anton for years. He lost the one person he loved, and Anton will not stop until others experience the same agony he feels. Tina is the instrument he will use for his vengeance, and before he is finished with his plans, Anton will make sure that the EOD is ripped apart.

*Carl Monroe*—A conscience has never gotten in Carl's way. He's a cold-blooded killer, and remorse isn't something that he understands. A knife is his weapon of choice, and he does love using that weapon on his prey.

# Chapter One

"You're making a mistake!" Dr. Tina Jamison shouted as she was hauled out of the nondescript brown van and pushed into the dimly lit parking garage.

But the four men—all wearing black ski masks—didn't seem to care that they'd grabbed the wrong woman.

And they *had* gotten the wrong person. They must have made some kind of mistake. There was no way these armed gunmen could actually want *her.*

The man on the right jabbed his gun into her back. "Move!"

When someone shoved a gun at her, Tina knew exactly what to do. *Move.* Just as the man had ordered. But Tina was scared and she stumbled, nearly slamming face-first into the cement as she hurried to follow the guy's order.

*This can't be happening. This can't be happening.*

She'd been safe in her hotel room less than an hour ago. Sleeping. Minding her business.

She'd woken to find a man leaning over her. His hand had flattened over her mouth before she could scream. Then he'd put a gun to her head and told her that if she wanted to live, she'd follow his orders.

Tina wanted to keep living.

One of the men pushed open the stairwell door. Then the gun was poking into her back once more. Tina got the message loud and clear, and she started double-timing it up those concrete stairs.

*Why? Why have they taken me?* "Look, you've got the wrong girl." She tried telling them this fact for what had to be the fiftieth time. They needed to see reason and listen to her. "I'm a doctor, okay? Just a doctor who—"

"We know exactly who you are," the man with the gun replied in a hard, lethal voice. "And we know just what Mercer will pay to get you back."

Her blood iced as Tina grabbed for the stair railing. Mercer. Oh, no. With the mention of Bruce Mercer's name, the situation went from bad to unbelievably, terribly worse. Because Bruce Mercer was the director of a covert group of agents who conducted secret missions for the United States' government. Bruce Mercer operated the EOD, the Elite Operations Division.

Bruce Mercer was also her boss.

*But I'm not an agent! I'm a doctor! The one who patches up the wounded after a battle.*

Because Tina had learned long ago that she didn't mix so well with danger.

Her heart was about to gallop out of her chest right then and, taking a breath— Oh, yes, it was hard. Painful. She was very afraid that she might be about to hyperventilate. Her breath sure seemed to be wheezing out with each frantic exhale.

"Can you…" Tina huffed. "Move the gun?" If the guy stumbled, that gun could accidentally discharge. She knew firsthand the kind of severe damage a shot to the spine would do to a victim.

"No, I can't." The gun jabbed harder into her.

"Look, I—I…" She tried to suck in air. *Don't panic. Don't.* "I'm not who you think I am!" She wasn't an EOD agent. If these men were taking her because they mistakenly thought that she had some kind of classified information she could give to them, they were dead wrong. She didn't have the clearance level needed to access that sort of intel.

"We know you're not an agent," the man snapped. "Now keep climbing. *Faster.*"

She climbed until her legs burned. Flight after flight. Finally a door opened above her. The scent of fresh air and the mighty Mississippi River teased her nose as Tina was led outside.

Stars glittered overhead. Glancing around, she realized they were on a rooftop. And…and she could hear the *whoop-whoop-whoop* of an approaching helicopter.

*This is so not good.* As if masked men with guns could be good. But any group that came equipped with their own helicopter sure equaled a whole world of trouble in her book.

Fear had Tina shaking, but she made herself turn to face the gunman. "I-if you know I'm not an agent…" She had to raise her voice, nearly shouting, to be heard over the helicopter's approach. The wind from its blades blew against her, and she trembled. "If you know that, then let me go! I'm of no use to you."

The masked man—the fellow had to be the leader because no one else had done any talking—shook his head. "Mercer's daughter is going to be plenty of use to us."

Mercer's daughter? Tina's eyes widened. Definitely the wrong person. "I'm not his daughter!"

A rough, twisted bark of laughter escaped from the gunman. "Sure you aren't, sweetheart." A Texas accent. She could just hear it slip around his words. "That's why Mercer pays for your apartment in D.C. and why he sprung for the fancy hotel here in New Orleans. Why he's been paying your bills for years." More laughter. "At first, I thought you might be his lover, and that connection would have been just as useful to me."

The helicopter circled around to land. Her abductors had given her time to dress—a humiliating task since they'd watched her every move. The wind from the landing helicopter made her T-shirt cling tightly to her chest and it tossed her hair wildly around her face.

"Then I got intel that revealed your true identity." He let the gun trail over her cheek. If she *had* been an agent, Tina would have done something incredibly cool right then. Such as wrestle the gun from him or give him a sharp right hook.

Then take *all* of these jerks out.

But she wasn't an agent. She knew how to heal, not how to hurt.

"You've been the one constant in Mercer's life since you got out of med school. You're that constant because you're Bruce Mercer's daughter. The daughter he tried to hide after your mother was killed in that attack in France."

She swallowed. The fact that she'd been born in France was really going to work against her here.

"Of course, if you're not his daughter, you can just prove that to me."

The gun was still at her cheek.

The helicopter's blades had stopped.

"Prove who you really are," the man in the mask murmured. There were slits over his eyes so that he could see out, but the rest of his face was concealed. All she knew was that the guy was big, with narrow shoulders and hips, and that his words carried a slight Texas accent. She couldn't physically identify *any* of the men who had taken her.

"Are we ready?" another voice called out as heavy footsteps approached from behind her. This voice didn't hold a Texas accent. This one just sounded bored.

It also sounded familiar.

Tina felt her cheeks turn ice-cold, then they burned red hot.

Those footsteps kept approaching. "Yeah, we got our package," the gunman said with a quick nod. "Though she's been whining the whole time about us having the wrong woman."

The weapon finally left her cheek. Moving slowly, carefully, because she sure didn't want to set anyone off, Tina turned to face the man. The helicopter waited behind him, perched perfectly in place.

There was a ski mask over this man's face, too. Slits for his eyes, a hole for his mouth. As the others, he was also dressed in black from head to toe.

But she *knew* him; knew those broad shoulders, the tall, tough build. He towered over the other men by several inches and he walked with a slow, stalking grace.

Relief swept through her and Tina felt dizzy. *Drew Lancaster.*

"If she's been talking so much…" his familiar voice rolled over her, edged with a Mississippi drawl, "then maybe you should have just gagged her."

Wait. *What?* Tina's eyes widened in horror. That wasn't what Drew was supposed to say. Drew wasn't a criminal. He was a good guy. He was a federal agent with the EOD.

He moved behind her, and put his hand over her mouth. "See?" Drew murmured. "Easy enough to stop her from talking."

She nearly bit him.

But Drew bent and put his mouth right next to her ear. "Stay calm." A bare whisper. One Tina wasn't even sure she hadn't imagined. But she'd felt the warm rush of his breath against her ear and a shiver slid through her body.

Drew kept his hand over her mouth as his head lifted a

few inches. His eyes glittered down at her. She knew those eyes were golden, the color of a jungle cat that she'd seen once in the D.C. zoo.

Drew had always reminded her of that great cat. Because he was wild and dangerous, and he'd scared her, on an instinctive level, from the first moment they'd met.

"I didn't realize our cargo tonight was a woman," Drew charged as he glanced over at the lead gunman. "Maybe next time, you should clue me in on that."

The guy grunted. "Need-to-know basis, Stone. Need to know." Then he jerked his thumb toward the chopper. "Now are you ready to get us out of here?"

*Stone.* Her lips pressed against Drew's palm. She hadn't seen him in two months. Not since he'd left for his last mission.

Drew shifted his body and glanced down at her. This time, Tina could see past her fear and she easily read the hard warning in his eyes.

Drew was undercover. These men—they knew him as someone named Stone.

And something else that Tina realized... Drew wasn't about to blow his cover.

Not for her.

Her shoulders slumped. Things were going to get even worse before they got better.

"I'm ready," Drew said. He dropped his hand and backed away from her.

The gun was jabbed into her back once more. She didn't tense this time.

But Drew did. "Is that necessary?" The words seemed gritted.

"Yeah, it is. Now get that bird off the ground!"

Drew's gaze dropped to the gun then his stare slid back to Tina. She knew that she had to look terrified.

Because she was.

"Do you seriously think she's going to get away?" Drew glanced around the rooftop. "No one's up here but us."

The gun didn't move.

"Her hands are tied. She's not going any place." Drew exhaled. "And I don't see—"

"She's Bruce Mercer's daughter!" the gunman snarled. "You think he didn't train her? Until we're clear, I'm keeping my weapon on her."

Drew blinked. "Bruce Mercer's daughter," he repeated softly, considering the information it appeared.

*No, I'm not!*

But did Drew know that?

"I guess that changes things," Drew said. Then he turned away and hurried back to the chopper without even a second glance. In seconds, all of the men had climbed in behind him and Tina found herself secured in the backseat.

The blades were spinning again, matching the frantic beat of her heart, and the helicopter rose high into the air.

HIS COVER WAS about to be blown to hell and back.

Drew Lancaster slowly lowered the chopper onto the landing pad. His jaw was locked tight, his hands held the controls securely and rage beat at his insides.

*Tina Jamison.*

When he'd landed the bird on that roof, the pretty little doctor had sure been the last person he'd expected to see. But she'd spun toward him, her eyes wide and desperate behind the lenses of her glasses, and he'd realized that he was in some serious trouble.

She'd known who he was. Without even seeing his face, Tina had known. Maybe his voice had given him away. He hadn't bothered to change accents with this particular group. He'd just wanted them to think he was a slow-talking, ex-soldier from Mississippi. A man with a grudge against the government. A man willing to do just about anything for cash.

Tina's face had lit with hope when she'd seen him. Such a beautiful face it was, too. He'd found himself admiring it more and more during his visits to the doc at the main EOD office. She'd been all business, of course, checking his vitals, talking to him about stress in the field.

He'd been imagining her naked.

Before the blades had stopped spinning, Lee Slater was already out of the chopper and dragging Tina with him. The jerk still had that gun far too close to her for Drew's peace of mind.

*How am I supposed to get her out of here?*

With narrowed eyes, Drew watched Tina and Lee vanish into the main house. More armed men followed them inside.

They were in the middle of Texas, at a dot on the map that most folks would never find. It wasn't as if the cops were just going to rush in and rescue the kidnapped woman.

He was deep undercover. Working under the alias of Stone Creed. The men here—they were looking to cause as much chaos on U.S. soil as they possibly could. They were into drugs, into weapons and into wrecking the political powers that be.

And, in particular, it seemed that the men were looking to take out the EOD. Or, more specifically, they wanted to destroy Bruce Mercer.

Drew climbed from the chopper and checked his own gun.

"Can you believe it?" the excited voice asked from behind him.

Drew looked back just as Carl Monroe yanked off his ski mask. Yeah, that mask wasn't exactly necessary anymore. Not since they were back on their own turf. They didn't have to worry about unwanted eyes seeing them here.

Carl grinned. "We got the EOD director's daughter!"

No, they hadn't. Drew swallowed. Bruce Mercer did have a daughter, all right, but that daughter wasn't Tina Jamison.

What would happen when the men realized that they'd taken the wrong woman?

*She will become a dead woman.*

He couldn't let that happen. He'd been sent in to gather intel on this group, to determine just how much of a threat the individuals known as HAVOC posed—and, once his assessment had been made, his team was supposed to eliminate that threat.

It sure looked as if his timetable had just been accelerated.

"She sure is pretty," Carl said. Like Lee, Carl was a Texas boy, born and bred. He was also very, very dangerous. Carl liked to use his knife—often. And, according to his file, Carl enjoyed watching his victims slowly die from their knife wounds. Torture and pain were all part of Carl's twisted package.

"You should have seen her," Carl continued, voice thickening, "when we found her in that hotel room. She was all tousled and—"

Drew whirled on him. "Are you going to help me secure the chopper?" His words rapped out. Fury had coiled in his gut. No way, no damn way, should Tina have been put at risk like this. At his first opportunity, he had to contact the other EOD agents assigned to the HAVOC mission. They needed to work an immediate extraction on her.

And if they didn't, then he would.

Carl's smile stretched. "You thought she was pretty, too, didn't you? It's those glasses… Sexy."

He wanted to drive his fist into Carl's face.

But Carl turned away and went to work on the chopper.

Drew exhaled slowly as he tried to bring his control back in check. He was still the new guy in this crew. Useful because he could fly anything—and kill anyone instantly. Sure, his dossier had been faked, but his skills were plenty real enough.

During his time in Delta Force, Drew had been turned into a lethal fighting machine. He didn't need a weapon to take out a dozen men. He could do that just with—

A scream cut the night. *Her* scream.

Drew was running toward the main house before he could even think about his response.

The door was shut, so he just kicked his way right through it. The wood banged against the wall.

*"Don't!"* Tina yelled. "Please, I—"

Her cry was abruptly cut off.

Drew felt the familiar ice encase his fury. That was the way it had always been for him. When it came time for a battle, he went ice-cold. No emotion. No room for mistake.

He'd been called a robot by some of his teammates before.

He'd been called a hell of a lot worse by his enemies.

*Why had Tina stopped screaming?*

Another door was in front of him. A tall, blond guy with a gun at his hip tried to block Drew's path. "Stone, man, I don't think they want you right now."

Drew shoved the guy out of his way. He went *in* that room.

The first thing he saw was the blood. Fat drops that were sliding down Tina's arm. Lee Slater stood next to her, a knife in his hand. "I think that's what we need."

In his mind, Drew saw himself rushing across the room and breaking the guy's wrist. The knife would clatter to the floor, falling from Lee's slack fingers. With him out of commission, Drew would turn on the other two men there. He could have them all on the floor in less than a minute.

But he didn't attack. Not yet. Because he'd been given very specific orders from Bruce Mercer.

The job was top priority. The fear was that these men—men from the U.S., from Mexico and from parts of South America—had access to classified government intel. There had been a leak at the EOD just months before, and they were still tracking to determine just how much information had been taken from headquarters.

They'd followed the trail to HAVOC. Drew was supposed to be days away from meeting the group's leader.

*Days.*

Getting an up-close audience with the man named Anton Devast wasn't an easy task. Those who got close usually wound up getting killed.

Drew locked his jaw. "Why'd you cut her?"

They'd cut Tina *and* gagged her. The gag would explain why she'd stopped screaming. Damn it, the gag had been his suggestion, but he'd only said it to clue her in to the fact that she needed to stay quiet about him.

Her eyes—so green and bright—found his. There was a desperate plea in her gaze.

A plea that he couldn't answer right then. Not if they wanted to both keep living.

"I was just showing her," Lee said softly, "what would happen if she tried to escape. We can treat her well…" He lifted the knife. Blood coated the blade. "Or we can make this little stay turn into her worst nightmare."

A tear leaked down Tina's cheek. She had high cheekbones, a slightly pointed chin and the cutest damned nose with its spray of freckles.

Normally her face was full of soft color and life.

Right then, fear had etched its way across her face. He didn't like for Tina to be afraid. Not one bit.

"You showed her," Drew growled. "She got the message. Now put the knife up."

Lee's dark eyes narrowed. "I don't take orders from you."

Fine. Drew stalked toward him. He grabbed the guy's wrist. *Don't break it, not yet.* But the threat was there, and Lee would know it. "You think the boss would like it if you killed Mercer's daughter? Seems to me she's a tool that he can use. Not something to be damaged."

Lee swallowed. The guy liked giving pain, but he couldn't handle being on the receiving end of it. He was also afraid of Drew, mostly because Drew had gotten into HAVOC by fighting his way in. He'd taken down five men, left them bloody and broken. The initiation had been hell.

But so was life.

"It's just a cut," Lee said dismissively. "No big deal."

"Don't cut her again. If the boss wanted her, then the boss will get her." Maybe he could use that. Surely, Devast would want to come in for a personal look at Mercer's daughter.

That visit would give Drew his chance to eliminate the man.

After all, eliminating Anton Devast was his job. At his core, Drew was a killer.

Still holding Lee, Drew let his gaze return to Tina. He didn't like seeing tears in her eyes.

And—her glasses were cracked. He let his hold on Lee tighten a little more. "I'll take first watch on her," Drew said.

Lee was trying to yank his hand free. Failing. "What?"

He hadn't stuttered. "I'll take first watch." Because he didn't trust anyone else with her. Definitely not Lee or Carl.

Lee's eyes were angry slits, but he gave a grim nod. "Fine, you do that." His short, red hair looked as if he'd raked his fingers through it. "You can stay with her while I get some sleep."

He made his words sound like an order. Whatever. As long as the guy got out of there...

Drew released the man.

It only took an instant for Lee's smirk to come back. "I'll see you again soon, sweetheart," he promised Tina. His gaze flickered to Drew. "And I'll see you later, too, Stone." A threat hung in the words.

He'd have to stay extra alert. The way Lee was eyeing him, Drew knew he might find a knife shoved into his own ribs during an unguarded moment.

Not like that would be the first time.

Drew lifted his hand and his fingers traced over the thick scar on his right cheek. "You sure will." He made certain that his words held just as much of a threat as Lee's had.

Actually they held *more* of a threat. Showing a weakness with these guys was a mistake, because they'd most definitely attack that weakness.

Drew didn't move until Lee and his two cronies were out of the room. When the door shut behind them, he exhaled slowly.

Tina was still staring at him with her wide, desperate eyes.

He wanted to tell her that everything was going to be okay, but he couldn't be sure listening devices weren't in the room. When he'd first reached the compound, he'd found two bugs in his bunk room.

It only figured that there would be some in there, too.

He glanced toward the door. Even though Drew had said that he'd take first watch, Lee might have stationed a guard outside.

"Mumph."

His attention slid back to Tina.

"Mumm-mph…" She jerked in the chair. Someone had tied her to the chair. Probably Lee.

He crossed to her side and knelt on the floor so that they'd be at eye level. "The ropes were tied too tight," he muttered, feeling anger try to push past his control once more.

*Can't have that. Must maintain cool.*

The other agents had him all wrong. They thought he was made of ice. That he didn't feel when he went out on his missions.

The problem was that he felt too much. And if he didn't control his fury… *Then I'm too dangerous.*

He loosened her binds. He glanced up at her, his gaze colliding with hers.

A crack ran across the right lens of her glasses, looking like a spider's web. He reached up.

She flinched.

"Easy," Drew murmured. "I'm just checking you out."

He lifted the glasses away from her face.

She blinked at him.

Hell. She was just as sexy without the glasses as she was with them. He'd thought maybe it was just a hot-librarian-type thing working for him, but no. The woman was simply temptation.

He didn't need temptation. He had a job to do.

*She's the job right now.* The words whispered from within him.

He put her glasses on the nearby table.

*"Mumph!"* Ah, now Tina was sounding angry behind the gag. He wasn't sure what would be better for her. Fear or anger. Unless they were careful, both might just get her killed.

He leaned toward her. Brought his mouth right to her ear just as he'd done before. Her scent, light, sweet strawberries, wrapped around him.

Because of Tina, he'd developed one serious addiction to strawberries over the past year. Not that she knew it. Not that she knew *anything* about him. To her, he was just another agent.

Another adrenaline junkie that she had to patch up and keep alive.

Only now it was his turn to keep her alive.

"Be very careful what you say," he barely breathed the words against the delicate shell of her ear.

Tina shivered.

Was that shiver from fear? Had to be. In these circumstances, he was foolish to think it could be from anything else.

But, just in case, he filed that reaction away for future notice. Because he'd sure like to know every sensitive spot on Tina's gorgeous body.

"They could be listening." His mouth brushed across her ear.

She gave the faintest of nods.

Her smell was incredible.

*Focus.*

He lifted his hands and undid the gag. The cloth dropped from her mouth.

Tina licked her lips and sucked in a deep gulp of air. "Thank you."

His own mouth tightened. She shouldn't be thanking him. He hadn't saved her. "I'm going to patch up your arm."

She blinked once more, and her gaze found his. She was still breathing deeply, gulping in air as if she'd been starved for it.

Her skin was porcelain pale and he wanted color staining her cheeks once more. He wanted the fear gone from her eyes.

*Trust me.* He mouthed the words to her.

After the faintest of hesitations, Tina nodded.

The ice melted a little around him. He turned away from her. Fumbled through the drawers in the room until he found some first-aid supplies. The men—and women—at the compound were always ready for battle, so that meant they had to be ready for the cleanup after that battle. He'd quickly learned that there were first-aid supplies scattered all around the place.

Tina didn't wince when he began to clean her wound with an antiseptic cloth. "It's not deep enough for stitches," he said as he put the bandage on her arm. "You're lucky."

Both her brows shot up.

Fine. So "lucky" hadn't been the best word to describe her current situation.

He grabbed a chair and pulled it toward her. She was still tied up, and he had to keep her that way or the others would wonder what the hell was happening. "You're going to be all right."

Tina's gaze just stared back at him.

He realized that she didn't believe him. Maybe that was good—because Drew hated making promises he couldn't keep.


"Mr. Mercer?"

Bruce Mercer looked up from the files that were spread across his desk. His assistant, Judith Rogers, stood in the doorway. Judith hated buzzing him. She'd said once that buzzing was too impersonal for her, and she usually came in to tell him when he had a visitor.

So her standing there…walking in unannounced…that wasn't unusual.

The fear in Judith's eyes *was* unusual.

"Tina Jamison is missing," Judith told him as she twisted her hands into fists. "I just got the call from an agent at her hotel. The lock on her door was broken, and Tina—she's gone."

Mercer didn't let the expression on his face alter.

This situation had been one that he feared. He was playing a deadly game, and Tina could have just become a pawn in that game.

If he wasn't careful, he might lose his pawn.

He might lose the whole damn game.

"Get me Dylan Foxx," Mercer demanded. "Right *now.*" Because he was going to need agents in the field to work this case and to make sure that Tina survived the battle that was coming.

He'd foolishly positioned Tina right in the middle of that battle.

*I'm sorry, Tina.*

He didn't make mistakes often, but when he did…they were deadly.

# Chapter Two

"It's time for me to take over." The gruff voice had Tina's head jerking up.

She'd actually fallen asleep. How was that even possible? Tina blinked bleary eyes and found herself staring at Drew.

He was right in front of her. His gaze held hers an instant, then he turned his head and looked at the guy who'd just come into the room.

Tina had no idea who this blond man was. As he watched her, his hard brown eyes glittered. There was a holster at his hip—she could see the butt of his gun. And he had a knife strapped to his left side.

After her last encounter with a knife, Tina wasn't exactly eager to go another round with a blade.

"Lee said for me to relieve you," the man said in that same gruff voice. He shrugged. "So here I am."

Tina wanted to reach out and hold tight to Drew, but that wasn't possible.

Mostly because she was still tied up, but at least the gag was gone. That horrible, terrible gag. If she hadn't gotten her medicine just a few hours before the men had taken her, she wouldn't have been able to handle the gag. Tina wouldn't have been able to breathe.

"Keep that knife in its sheath, Carl," Drew told him flatly.

Oh, no. Oh, that wasn't *good.*

Drew's face—handsome, hard, fierce—seemed to tighten even more as he studied the other man.

Drew Lancaster was a warrior. She knew it. Had known it from the first moment she'd seen him. He'd been dripping blood at the time, courtesy of a fresh bullet wound. He hadn't even flinched when she'd dug that bullet out of him.

He was big; about six foot three, with wide shoulders, narrow hips and what she thought of as a go-to-hell golden gaze. His skin was tanned from hours under the Mississippi sun, and that slow drawl that crept out every now and then...

That drawl was temptation in a dangerous package.

She knew how lethal Drew was. She'd gotten a glimpse into his file once, thanks to her friend Sydney Ortez. Sydney controlled all the intel at the EOD, and when she'd noticed that Tina was spending a bit too much time gazing after Drew, Syd had wanted Tina to know exactly who she was day dreaming about.

Not a white knight.

More like a killing machine.

Drew's gaze slid to her once more. His face was all tough angles and planes. The scar that cut across his right cheekbone just made him appear all the more dangerous.

Her breath felt too hot in her lungs.

After a tense moment Drew gave a curt nod and rose to his feet. There was a tiny window in the room and sunlight spilled inside that window. The light fell on Drew as he passed it.

"Told you she was pretty," the one he'd called Carl mumbled.

Drew leaped at the other man. In an instant Drew's lower arm was under the guy's chin and Drew had him pinned against the wall. "And I'm telling you...*keep your hands off her.*"

The other man blinked. Then Carl smiled. "Like that, huh? Calling her yours already?"

*I am in a nightmare.* And Drew wasn't calling her anything.

But he was leaning in even closer to the blond male. "If you hurt her, if you so much as bruise her, I'll make you pay." A deadly promise.

The blond man gulped. "No worries, man. I'm just watchin' her."

Drew stepped back. "See that you do." He fired one more glance at Tina.

She had to press her lips together so she wouldn't cry out and basically beg him to stay.

He was undercover. He had a job to do. But she knew that he'd get her out of there.

She just had to hold on long enough for the rescue to work.

Drew turned and left the room without another word.

Carl eased toward her. "Guess you two got cozy, huh? Figured old Stone was a secret ladies' man."

He dropped into the chair near her. His hand went to the hilt of his knife.

Tina tensed, but he made no move to pull out the weapon.

His gaze swept over her face. "Such a pity," he murmured. "I hate it when pretty girls have to die."

HE WAS TAKING a risk. A huge one, Drew knew it, but he had to make the call. He slipped away from the others at the compound and headed toward the old fence on the right side of the property. He'd scouted before, and this was the weak spot in security. No cameras could see this location, but, thank goodness, there was actually cell service here.

Sydney Ortez had been the one to tell him about this sweet spot. Before Drew had gone in undercover, Sydney had used her satellites and her computer magic to try to find him a safe contact zone.

Safe, but not one hundred percent secure. Because in a situation such as this one, you never knew when the enemy might decide to take a stroll and blow your plans to hell.

Drew fired a quick glance over his shoulder. The phone was clutched tightly to his ear. One ring...

"I know about your problem," the voice on the other end of the line said. No identification was necessary. Drew instantly recognized the voice of his team leader, Dylan Foxx. The former SEAL had been the one to convince Drew to join the EOD in the first place. The two men had become old friends on the battlefield, on missions that they'd never discuss. So many years—so many missions. Through them all, Dylan always had Drew's back.

"Yeah?" Drew surveyed the area around him, trying to make sure no one was close enough to hear him. "So what the hell are we going to do?"

"Keep her alive," Dylan responded instantly. "Mercer knows what's happening. He says that Dr. Jamison's survival is priority."

Mercer knew. Right. The guy had eyes and ears everywhere.

*I'm a set of eyes and ears for him now.* "Does he realize I'm the one undercover here?"

"He does, and he said that you should make certain you stick to the doctor."

"They think she's his daughter," Drew stressed. How long would they keep working under that wrong assumption? How long until someone figured out they'd screwed up?

There was silence from Dylan, then he asked, "Is she?"

No. But Drew didn't give that immediate response. He trusted Dylan, of course he did, but there were some secrets he couldn't share.

Drew was one of the few people in the world who knew that, yes, Bruce Mercer actually did have a daughter. But that daughter wasn't Tina. "Hell if I know," he said.

It was a good thing Dylan wasn't there to see him. The guy had always said that he could read any lie on Drew's face. Lucky for Drew, the bad guys didn't have such an easy time of seeing past his deception.

"Tina Jamison wasn't supposed to be involved in this case," Drew growled. "No way. Who messed up? How did this happen?" Tina wasn't the bait for the trap they needed.

"I don't know." He could hear the frustration in Dylan's voice. "That's why I asked if she actually *is* his daughter, because that's the only thing making sense on my end. We gave Devast's men the false trail. They were supposed to follow it to *our* operative, not to Dr. Jamison."

Something had gone wrong. Very wrong. Now Drew had to stop the train wreck before Tina was killed.

There was a murmur in the background then Dylan said, "Get back to her. Word just came down that someone is about to send proof of life to the EOD."

Drew ended the call and started back toward the main house. Proof of life could be anything. Providing proof was the standard deal in an abduction case. That proof could be a video of the prisoner. A phone call from the captive.

It could be a severed finger. An ear that had been sliced off. That kind of physical evidence was actually often needed. High-profile prisoners were valuable and, before they were ransomed, their DNA had to be confirmed.

He couldn't let anyone cut into Tina.

He checked his weapon. Fully loaded.

Then he kicked up his speed and raced frantically back to Tina.

THE REDHEAD WAS BACK. Tina stared up at him—no, she stared into the guy's phone. He'd turned the phone sideways; he was video-taping her.

"This is what we call proof of life," he murmured. "We need you to prove to your dear old dad that you're still alive."

They weren't proving anything to her father. Her father *was* dead. So was her mother. They'd both died shortly after Tina's eighteenth birthday.

Their blood had soaked her fingers. She hadn't known how to save them.

*I do now.*

"Look into the camera," he ordered her. "Say your name."

The door opened behind him. Drew. Drew was back.

It got easier for her to breathe then.

She stared toward the redhead and his phone. "My name is Tina Jamison."

"Good girl," the redhead murmured. *Lee.* That was his name. She'd heard one of the other men call him that earlier. "Now tell us the date."

She did. Her voice didn't tremble. Tina was proud of that fact.

"Bruce Mercer, we have your daughter," the redhead said. His voice was cold and flat. "She's alive right now, but, if you don't follow our orders *exactly,* she won't be alive for long."

Tina kept staring at him.

"We want an exchange," Lee continued. "Her life for yours."

That wasn't going to happen. Not ever. Mercer was too important. He had ties to too many governments, too many agents, too many secrets.

She was just the doctor who patched up the team members.

*I'm expendable.*

Bruce Mercer wasn't.

"For every day that you delay, we will hurt her."

Oh, wait. *What?*

"We gave you proof of life," he continued. Her eyes narrowed. Was he recording these images of her? Or streaming them live to Mercer? If the fool was streaming them, the EOD would be on top of this group in hours. Sydney would trace the signal back to this location.

His hold tightened on the phone. "Now it's time for proof of pain."

He'd barely even got the words out before the other guy—the blond who'd kept her terrified for the past hour—came at her with his knife.

Tina tensed, but the knife just went to the ropes that bound her. Carl cut through the ropes that circled her right hand.

"What the hell…" Drew began.

"Slice off her finger," was the order that followed.

Carl smiled.

Tina tried to jerk her hand back.

She couldn't. He was too strong.

"Stop!" Drew bellowed.

He wasn't stopping. The knife pressed toward her hand.

Tina looked away.

But the blade didn't slice her skin. Instead she heard

the brutal thud of two bodies colliding. Her head whipped back toward that sound. Drew had just slammed into Carl. He'd tackled him, and both men had hit the floor. The knife clattered away.

"What are you doin', Stone?" Finally, Lee had dropped his phone. The video show seemed over.

Drew pounded Carl's head into the floor. Then he leaped to his feet. "You aren't cutting her, Lee."

"I'll do anything I want!" His chin jutted out, and Lee motioned to the other two men who stood against the back wall. "Take that fool down."

They ran toward Drew.

But they were the ones that hit the floor.

As he fought, Tina began to yank at the ropes still around her. Now that her right hand was free, she could escape. Her fingers were shaking as she undid the knots on her left hand. Then she started jerking at the ropes that tied her feet to the legs of the chair.

Grunts filled the room. The crunch of bones. The fight was brutal and—

More men were rushing inside.

Drew put his body in front of hers.

She untied the last knot and jumped to her feet.

"You aren't hurting her!" Drew shouted.

Then she heard a new sound. A very, very loud boom. A gunshot.

Drew's body jerked at the impact, but he didn't stop fighting the men who came at him. Of course, he didn't stop.

*A killing machine.*

He took down another man. Broke the nose of the fourth guy who rushed at him.

Hard hands grabbed Tina. A gun was shoved against her temple. Then Lee ordered, "Stop!"

Drew whirled. His gaze dipped to Tina's face, then back to the face of the gunman—Lee. "You aren't killing her," Drew said. His lips twisted into a humorless grin, one that was ice-cold. "She's no good to you dead."

"True." The gun lifted away from her. "Though it seems that *you* are no good to me alive."

He was going to shoot Drew again. Kill him while she watched. *"No!"* Tina yanked free of Lee's arms with a wild burst of strength. She put her body in front of Drew's. "Don't!"

Lee hesitated. His gaze went from her face back to Drew. "Interesting."

"I'll cooperate," she said, desperate because more men had run into the room. Alerted by the sounds of battle, they'd rushed inside. Now she and Drew were surrounded by guns and by men who looked as though they were ready to fire those guns at any moment. "I'll do whatever you want. I'll get my…father to meet your demands." Such a lie. "But, please, don't hurt him."

Carl had dragged himself off the ground. Blood dripped from his busted lower lip. "T-told you," he stuttered to Lee. "Stone here got sweet on the girl during his night duty."

"I think it's more than that," Lee said. A shrewd understanding filled his eyes. "Get some cuffs. Snap 'em on him." His head cocked to the right. "Cuffs will hold him better than rope." Then his lips lifted into a cold grin. "Even better, cuff him to *her*."

So much for keeping his cover in place. He'd sure blown that fast enough.

As soon as that knife had come close to her fingers, he'd attacked.

*Where was the ice?* When the knife had hovered over

her delicate hand, rage had ignited within him, driving right past his control.

The cuffs bit into his wrists. He wasn't surprised they'd used cuffs on him instead of rope. But when it came to thinking that the cuffs would be more secure than the rope, Lee was dead wrong.

They'd taken him and Tina into another room, a smaller room, with no window and sealed with a heavy, metal door. They'd cuffed one of his hands to hers, and his other hand—they'd cuffed it to a metal pole that came straight out of the floor.

Carl smirked at him. "That will hold you until it's time for us to play."

*Play.* Right. Wonderful.

Lee stood in the doorway behind Carl. "You know, Stone, there was something about you that I never liked."

Carl drove his fist into Drew's gut. He grunted. The jerk sure knew how to deliver some pain with a hard punch.

Lee sauntered into the room. He pushed Carl back and glared at Drew. They'd taken Drew's weapons. They'd also given him plenty of punches in the other room, despite Tina's pleas for them to stop.

They weren't exactly the type to show mercy. He didn't expect any.

"You've got secrets, don't you, Stone?" Lee said. His left brow rose. "If that's even your name."

Drew smiled. "You know you're a dead man."

Lee's lashes flickered. The flash of fear was obvious as the guy stepped back.

"I'm sending the video to Mercer. The video of his daughter…and the video of you, getting your butt beat."

Drew shrugged. "I don't think Mercer will care that some jerk he doesn't know was attacked."

"Maybe. Or maybe…just maybe…he does know you." Lee's gaze cut to Tina. "You made a mistake."

Saving her? No, it hadn't been a mistake. Saving her had been worth every second of pain.

"You looked at her with a lover's eyes, and you've never looked at anyone like that before."

Every muscle in Drew's body stiffened. Lee wasn't as dumb as he looked. *He's too observant.*

"I've seen you with plenty of women. You play around, you drink, and you don't care what they do when you're done." Half of Lee's mouth hitched up in a taunting smile. "But when you looked at her, when you burst into that room and saw me cutting her, your eyes were different. *I saw you.*"

This was bad.

"And you went crazy when I let old Carl loose on her."

He forced his back teeth to unclench. "Carl shouldn't be turned loose on any woman."

"She's not just any woman, is she? You know her."

Tina wasn't speaking beside him. But he could hear the sounds of her breaths, coming far too fast.

Then Lee advanced toward her. He grabbed Tina's chin. "And you know him, don't you?"

"No!" Tina cried.

Drew could almost believe her denial.

Almost.

"Well, I'll find out. I'll send this message to Mercer, and then I'll be back to see just what secrets you have… you and Stone here. When I let Carl begin to cut him, I'm betting either he'll talk—" Lee's fingers tightened on her chin "—or you will."

"Leave her alone," Drew ordered.

Lee shook his head. "See, that's what I'm sayin'. You get too protective for a man who doesn't know her, and that makes me wonder... Just *how* do you know her? How would a man like you know Bruce Mercer's daughter?" Menace layered his voice. "Want to know what I'm suspecting?"

"Not really. I don't give a damn," Drew retorted. He just needed Lee and Carl to get out of there so he could escape and get Tina to safety.

"I think one of Mercer's agents would know her. I think you're a man with a certain set of skills, skills a guy like Bruce Mercer would appreciate."

"You're thinking way too hard," Drew told him. "Don't hurt yourself."

Lee's eyelids flickered. "Getting an agent in here, monitoring us...that would be a Mercer move," Lee continued as he stepped away from Tina. With a nod, he said, "Maybe you are the killer I thought you were—only you're killing for the U.S. government. Not for HAVOC."

Drew made himself smile. The bullet was still in his shoulder, and it hurt, throbbing and burning constantly. But he was used to ignoring pain, so he shoved that burn deep into the back of his mind. "If I am EOD, then you need to be watching your back. 'Cause *maybe*—" he deliberately tossed the word back at Lee "—I got a team here, backing me up. *Maybe* this little place of yours is about to explode around you."

No, it wasn't. Drew's team wasn't close enough for that fast of an attack. They wouldn't even realize he'd been compromised at this point.

But Lee didn't know he was bluffing. And all of a sudden the guy started to sweat as worry sank in deep. "We need to sweep the perimeter!" Lee said as he spun toward Carl. "I have to make sure the place is secure."

With the big boss coming in, the guy wouldn't want any screw-ups.

Lee grabbed Carl's shirt. "You get outside that door. You make sure that no one enters and no one leaves until I get back." His hold tightened on Carl. "I trust you. You came up with me through the ranks."

How wonderful for them. Drew's eyes narrowed as he filed that little piece of information away for later.

"In case this jerk has any other teammates here undercover, I want *you* securing him. No one but me comes in here, got it?" Lee demanded.

Carl nodded. "Got it."

After firing one last fuming glare at Drew, the two men marched from the room. The door slammed and Drew heard the distinct sound of the lock setting into place.

"I'm sorry." Tina's voice was hoarse.

He grunted and yanked against the pole. He didn't have anything with him that he could use to pick the lock on the cuffs, so he had to find another means of escape. Yanking down the pole seemed like a fairly good option number two.

"The bullet is still in you, isn't it?"

"That's the least of our trouble." As soon as Lee realized that EOD agents weren't about to swarm the place, the guy would be back. He'd torture Drew then kill him, and Tina would get an up-close seat for that bloody show.

The pipe began to groan.

"What are you doing?"

Drew figured there was no point in sugarcoating things with her. "You know this is a torture room, right?"

Her breath rushed out.

"See the drain over there? It's so they can hose the place down when they're done and just wash the blood right away. Fast and easy cleanup." Lee had transferred them into that room so that he could fully take advantage of the facilities.

Lee had plans.

Drew was ready to destroy those plans.

"He should've checked the equipment," Drew said softly. "Sloppy mistake." Lee had probably cuffed other prisoners to this pole before to hold them in place.

But one thing Lee seemed to have missed...desperate prisoners struggled. The men and women that Lee had hurt in the past would have struggled desperately to escape from the pole—and the pain.

And their struggles had loosened the pole. It wasn't fully embedded in the hard floor any longer.

Perfect.

"Drop with me," Drew ordered in a low whisper. He didn't want Carl hearing them.

Without a word, Tina dropped with him. The floor was cold and hard, and it smelled of blood. Hell, he wanted her out of that place. No way did Tina belong in a room like this. He yanked again against the pole and then... then Tina was there, adding her strength to his. She'd positioned her body closer to his, and she was jerking on the pole with him.

It groaned again, and Drew stilled. "Wait." Because he didn't want to alert Carl, not yet.

But Carl didn't come rushing into the room.

"Again," Drew whispered.

They yanked again, and the pole lifted off the floor, just a few centimeters, but that was all Drew needed. He slid his cuff under the pole and his left wrist was free.

*Hell, yes.*

He jumped to his feet and Tina rushed up with him. "What about this one?" she said, tugging on the cuff that connected their wrists.

"That one's going to have to stay." Until he could find something to pick the lock or find a saw to cut the cuffs off. And if she was going to stay cuffed to him, then Tina needed to realize… "We're going to be targets."

Her eyes were wide. Stark.

*No glasses.*

He swore. "Just how much can you see?"

"I'm fine. I'm near-sighted, so I can see up close pretty much perfectly."

Which should work, since she had to stay up-close with him.

"I'll be your eyes for distance," he said.

She licked her lips and, of course, that just made his gaze drop to her mouth.

*Focus.*

He exhaled slowly and let the ice sweep over him. "You follow my every order, understand? No hesitations, no questions. Because a hesitation will get you—or both of us—killed."

She nodded. Her dark hair brushed over her shoulders.

"These are bad men, Tina." Bad was an understatement. "You know what they want to do to you." Cutting off her finger would just be the start of their fun.

Her gaze held his.

"So just be prepared for what I have to do…to them." Their escape wasn't going to be some walk in the park. It might even turn into a blood bath.

"What can I do?" She shook her head. "I want to help you, not just be some burden that you have to carry out of this place."

"Help by staying alive."

Her lips tightened. "That's not what I meant."

He knew, and Drew also knew that he didn't want to risk her. *But she will be risked.* There was no escaping the danger surrounding her. "How the hell did you even get in this mess?"

"I don't know."

His left hand lifted. The loose cuff dangled from his wrist. He touched her cheek.

Tina flinched.

"Easy." He wouldn't hurt her, ever. Didn't she realize that? "Before I open that door…" *And I run the chance of losing my life before I get the one thing I've wanted for so long…* "There's something I need to do."

A faint line appeared between her brows. "What?"

He was a bloody, bruised mess. When he'd imagined this moment—and he had, many times—it had been different.

Oh, well. So much for his best-laid plans.

"What?" Tina asked again.

"This." He put his mouth on hers. Drew had to do it. He had to find out if the woman would be as good in reality as she was in his dreams.

At first Tina didn't move at all. She'd frozen on him—maybe his ice had transferred to her.

Some dreams were better than reality. He began to pull away.

Then Tina leaned toward him. Her lips parted beneath his and she kissed him back with a wild, reckless passion he hadn't expected.

Some dreams couldn't touch reality.

He put his hand under her chin, aware of the weight of that dangling cuff. He tilted her head back so that he could plunder her mouth, so that he could taste her.

Hell, in that moment, he wanted to consume her.

His body ached for her. Need pulsed through his veins, and if they weren't in some pit of hell…if the bad guys weren't just down the hallway…

Drew lifted his head. "Then you'd be mine," he rasped.

Tina blinked and shook her head. "What?"

He kissed her once more, just because he had to do it. *There's no way we're dying.* The woman was full of secrets, and he'd be sure he had the chance to discover every single one. "I've wanted to do that since the first time I walked into your office and you told me to take off my shirt."

Her gorgeous eyes widened. "Your shirt was covered in blood."

As if a little matter of a bullet wound could have stopped him from wanting her. "It is now, too." *A bullet wound won't stop the need.* He rocked back on his heels. "Remember, no hesitation."

Her lips were swollen from his mouth. She was so sexy right then. Sexy, but still scared. Talk about terrible timing.

That was the story of his life.

He backed her up against the wall on the right side of the room. Drew calculated that this would be his best attack spot.

He rolled his shoulders, pushed down his fury. He had to take out his prey one at a time. First, Carl would go down. Carl who'd wanted to slice away one of Tina's fingers.

*Rage...* Drew swallowed and pushed the rage down again.

Carl would be taken out first. Then Drew and Tina would rush down the hallway. Another guard would be at the door that led outside. Maybe two guards would be there. Drew would have to take them out, too.

He and Tina would stay low, keeping to cover. There was a motorcycle waiting in the garage. One the others thought was out of commission, but that Drew had taken the time to ensure was actually fully operational.

He liked having backup plans available.

His muscles were tight, battle ready. Tina watched him with wide eyes.

*Protect her. Get her out.*

Once Tina was safe, he'd come back to finish this mission. *I have to eliminate Anton Devast.*

He gave a little nod. "Okay, Doc, it's show time." He
waited a beat, then said, "Scream for me."

She didn't scream.

Hadn't they talked about not hesitating? Drew was sure
that he'd gone over that part with her. "Scream!"

She screamed.

An instant later Carl rushed through the door.

## Chapter Three

Tina screamed. She screamed as loudly as she possibly could. She'd always had a rather good scream—horror-movie good—and her scream had Carl racing back into the room.

But her scream was cut off when Drew's fingers locked around her throat. "You're dead," he growled.

"What's goin' on here?" Carl demanded.

Drew's grip was strong, but not painful. The look in his eyes—that was terrifying. He should have given her a head's up about this little bad cop—uh, agent—routine.

"You ruined everything for me," Drew told her. "Everything."

"You can't hurt her!" Carl snapped. "That's what I'm doing—"

He grabbed for Drew's shoulder.

His mistake.

Drew swung toward him. The loose cuff on Drew's left wrist flew out and hit Carl in the face. Then Drew punched Carl in the face. A fast, brutal hit. Carl stumbled back. The weapon in his hand started to rise.

But Drew wasn't done. He chopped down with his hand, hitting Carl's arm, and the weapon fell from Carl's fingers.

A few more hits from Drew—Tina jerked forward

because when he moved, so did she—and Carl was on the floor.

His eyes were closed, and he was *out*.

Drew leaned over Carl and scooped up the gun. "Nice scream you got there, Doc."

And nice, brutal fighting skills he had there. Tina cleared her throat. "Ah, thank you."

He looked back over at her. "Ready?"

She nodded.

Drew led the way out of that prison. He eased open the room's door and peered down the hallway. She wondered if anyone else had heard her scream. No one else appeared to be racing toward them.

"Lee has most of the guys stationed outside. They're probably searching for my team." His voice was so quiet she had to strain to hear it.

*His team.* "When will they get here?" Hopefully, any moment. Then—

His gaze slid to hers. "They won't."

Her heart sank at that news.

"Don't worry, I've got you."

She would be more reassured when they were safely away from all of the bad guys with guns. Tina wanted to know who these guys were, why Drew was undercover there—what was happening!

But now wasn't the time for her questions. Now was the time to focus on survival—escape.

He searched the immediate area once more. "Clear." They rushed down the hall. Drew held the gun in his left hand. She'd known that he was ambidextrous; the man could wield a weapon just as easily with either hand. She'd watched him do just that on the shooting range once. That ambidextrous talent was a real good thing, since his right hand was still locked to her.

They approached another door—a heavy, wooden door.

"This will take us outside," he said, pausing briefly. "I don't want to use the bullets unless I have to because they'll just bring more company running toward us."

She wasn't in the mood for company, either.

He gave her the gun.

Wait. What?

"Use it, but only if you have to."

Then he opened the door. They slipped outside.

And a man with a gun immediately appeared in their path.

"Stone!" He glared at Drew. "You traitor! Lee warned me about you!" He brought up his gun.

Drew kicked out at the guy; his boot connecting with a snap. The gun went flying, and so did the man. His head slammed into the cement behind him.

"Got you!" a voice snarled from Tina's right, a bare moment before hard hands wrapped around her. Those hands tried to rip her away from Drew's side, but with the cuffs, that wasn't happening.

But the vicious pull did make Drew attack. He spun and struck out with his fist.

The attacker let her go, but only for an instant. Only so he could lunge at Drew.

*No.*

She hit the guy with the butt of her gun.

He went down with a groan.

Drew curled his cuffed fingers around hers. "Nice job, Doc. Now let's *go.*"

Because no one else had seen them, not yet. Darkness

had fallen once more, and the glittering stars were above them as they raced toward what looked like an old barn.

They stayed to the shadows. Drew stopped her several times, lifting his hand and freezing when a rustle of movement sounded.

Then they were in the barn. Only, Tina quickly realized, it was more of a garage than a barn. Broken-down cars waited inside. Rusty tools lined the wooden walls. And, from what she could see, there was no means of escape. This plan wasn't working. "We need the helicopter," she said, grabbing his arm. The helicopter was their best bet. They could fly right out of that place.

"The chopper's too secure," Drew softly replied as he pulled her toward a thick, dark tarp. "We wouldn't be able to fuel it and get out of here before every man in the area swarmed us."

A swarming sounded bad.

"This is what we need." He tossed the tarp aside.

She saw the curving body of a motorcycle. One that looked as if it had seen better days a very long time ago. "Uh, I'm not sure…"

He'd already climbed on the motorcycle, the movement, of course, propelling her forward.

Tina dug in her heels. "There are tools here. Maybe we can cut the cuffs." So what if most of the tools looked to be about ten years old? There could be a sharp saw in there, somewhere.

"Our priority is getting to freedom right now, before a patrol comes through here." His eyes glittered at her. "We don't have any more time to waste. Get on the bike."

"I don't see a helmet."

She heard voices then, rising from outside.

He heard them, too. His body tensed. "Get on the bike!"

She'd just broken the no-hesitation rule of his again. Tina jumped on the motorcycle just as someone threw open the door to the garage.

"What the hell?" the guy in the doorway demanded. "Stone?"

Drew revved the motorcycle's engine. Because of their linked hands, Tina had to stretch her arm out next to his and had to press her body intimately close.

"Hold on," Drew told her.

She already was. For dear life.

The bike leaped forward, heading straight for the man in the doorway. Tina clamped her lips together so that she wouldn't scream.

After all, there was no need for her to scream. The man in the doorway was doing plenty of screaming.

Then that man was diving out of the way. Drew drove the motorcycle right through the door and out into the night.

Wind whipped against Tina's body, her hair flying behind her and— Oh, *no,* she realized that she'd dropped the gun.

Not exactly the pro move of an agent.

But then, she wasn't an agent, and she needed both hands to hold tight to Drew because he wasn't heading for some nice, paved road.

He was heading straight for a fence. One that had barbed wire at the top.

"Uh, Drew…"

"Don't worry, Doc. I got this."

At least, that was what she thought he said. It was hard to tell for certain over the roar of the bike. They were going faster and faster and— Was that a ramp? No, no, that was just boards, propped up against the fence. He couldn't possibly ride up on those—

He could.

He did.

They hurtled over the fence, clearing the barbed wire with inches to spare, even as voices shouted behind them.

When the bike touched down, Tina nearly flew right off the cracked seat. Luckily, the handcuff—and her death grip on Drew—had her jerking right back down.

The motorcycle's wheels spun. Dirt flew in the air. But Drew righted the bike before they could crash.

They hurtled forward once more.

Bullets thudded into the ground behind them.

Drew didn't stop. He gunned the engine and they raced off into the night.

Tina clung tightly to him. *Breathe. Just breathe.* The nightmare had to end—sooner or later.


"WE HAVE A PROBLEM."

Dylan Foxx glanced up at those quiet words. Rachel Mancini stood just inside the doorway of the small office. Her dark hair fell in a perfect, straight line to her chin. Her eyes—a bright blue that always seemed to look through him—reflected worry.

Rachel didn't worry often. There wasn't much that *could* make the ex-Marine worry.

"Another one?" Dylan muttered as he yanked a hand through his hair. He'd just finished a second phone call with Bruce Mercer. The big boss was furious and demanding action.

It was time for the team to move. They couldn't give Drew any longer on his own.

"Drew didn't check in."

He sucked in a sharp breath at the news. Yeah, that counted as a problem. Dylan surged out of his chair. As he walked toward her, Rachel's shoulders seemed to stiffen.

She did that around him. Always tensing up. Always closing him out.

He locked his own jaw. "Maybe he was delayed. Maybe—"

"Drew's never missed a check-in. I waited ten minutes, and he didn't make contact." She shook her head. "And I picked up some radio noise—something is happening out there. All of the men were called to action."

Hell. Rachel had been monitoring the radio waves and transmission signals from the HAVOC compound, extra ears in case Drew got into trouble.

She wet her lips. "There's…something else."

Her tone told him this was even worse.

"Drew's tracker went off-line."

Every EOD agent in the field had a tracking device implanted just beneath the skin. In case the agent was taken by the enemy, Mercer wanted to be able to get a lock on the missing man or woman. The EOD didn't like to lose agents.

Dylan had no intention of losing a teammate, and a friend.

"Maybe it's a system error," he said, even though his gut told him otherwise.

"I checked in with the techs at the EOD. They said his signal was transmitting fine until an hour ago, then it went dead."

Hell. "And there's no tracker implanted on Dr. Jamison."

"No, she's not an agent. Mercer never saw a need for her to be monitored. She wasn't supposed to be at risk."

Now she'd been taken and Drew had gone off the grid.

They had to get into the field. ASAP. Dylan hated being away from the action, especially when his team needed him. Especially when—

His phone rang. He glanced down and swore when he saw the number. He knew they were about to have more problems coming their way. With his eyes on Rachel, he answered the call. "Foxx."

"I just sent you a file that you need to view immediately." The voice on the other end of the line was feminine, husky, and one that was used to giving orders. *Sydney Ortez.* When it came to EOD Intel, Sydney was the go-to girl. She was also Mercer's right-hand woman. If something was happening within the organization, Sydney knew about it.

The fact that Sydney was *supposed* to be out on maternity leave as she prepared for the birth of her twins—well, the fact that she was calling him meant that something serious had gone down.

He put Sydney on speaker and pulled up the file on his phone.

Tina Jamison's face filled the screen. Her eyes were wide with terror.

"Look into the camera," a hard voice ordered. Dylan couldn't see the speaker. He figured the voice probably belonged to the man recording the video. "Say your name."

"My name is Tina Jamison."

"Good girl," the guy murmured.

Her voice held fear. The same fear that filled her eyes. Tina wasn't supposed to be in the field. Her place was in the office.

And Dylan knew why. Mercer had briefed him during that second phone call. Told Dylan all of Tina's secrets.

"Tina Jamison is my *friend,*" Sydney said softly. "I want her back. The EOD wants her back."

"Bruce Mercer, we have your daughter," the rumbling voice said on the video then.

"Tina isn't his daughter," Sydney said at the same instant. "The kidnappers are mistaken about her identity.

When they realize that mistake, Tina will become expendable to them."

Rachel raised her dark brows. "They took the wrong bait," she said sadly.

Yes, they had. The EOD's careful plans had gone horribly wrong.

Before Dylan could reply to Rachel, the voice from the video was talking again. "We want an exchange," the man continued. "Her life for yours."

Dylan whistled. Mercer had suspected this would happen.

"For every day that you delay, we will hurt her."

Tina stared out of that video, her eyes wide. But, wait, did her gaze just flicker to the left? It looked as if some of the tension had eased from her shoulders.

"We gave you proof of life," the male voice said. "Now it's time for proof of pain."

Another man approached Tina. All Dylan could see was the guy's back, his blond hair and the knife in his hand.

"Oh, dear God," Rachel whispered.

"Slice off her finger," the grating voice ordered.

The knife lowered toward Tina's hand.

"Stop!" A familiar bellow. Drew's bellow.

But the knife didn't stop.

Tina looked away.

After that, all hell broke loose. Or, rather, Drew Lancaster broke loose. He leaped forward and attacked the blond. The video image twisted, flew sideways, and Drew pummeled the guy on the floor.

Then another image filled the screen. A man wearing a black ski mask stared straight ahead and said, "We have your daughter, Mercer, and we have one of your precious EOD agents. If you don't come for them, if you don't trade yourself, they'll both die. I can promise you, their deaths will be long and very, very painful."

The video ended.

Rachel slowly exhaled. "That would explain why Drew isn't making contact."

Because he'd had to blow his cover to protect Tina.

"There is no exchange," Sydney told them. No emotion had entered her voice. For a moment she almost reminded him of Drew. "You have to extract Tina and Drew, immediately. Backup agents will be sent down to assist your team."

"And the original mission?" He wasn't just going to let a domestic terrorist group walk away unscathed. If those SOBs escaped, thousands could die.

*Not on my watch.*

"Contain Devast's group. Local law enforcement has already been alerted, and they'll move on your command."

This was a mess. A terrible, dangerous mess. "What about the group's boss? If we just get the underlings, we don't stop Anton Devast." That was why Drew had gone in. To take down the real threat. Not just the lackeys.

"We'll work to make his men turn on him. If he isn't there, if we can't get Devast in this raid, then we'll use any prisoners that are taken against him."

But they might not turn on their boss. If they were afraid enough—or stupidly loyal enough—they wouldn't.

He ended the call with Sydney. He understood exactly what had been said and what hadn't.

The EOD wasn't like other government agencies. They didn't follow official protocols, and they didn't always tie up their cases with nice, neat little bows.

More often, their cases ended in bloodshed and death.

Their cases were the darkest. The most dangerous.

An extraction wouldn't be easy, and attacking that compound—that attack could turn into a full-on war.

"Are you ready?" Dylan asked Rachel. Because sometimes, it didn't take an army to fight a war.

It just took a few well-trained soldiers.

She nodded.

"Then let's do this." Before any more innocents were pulled into the fray.

HE'D LOST THEM, for the moment. That moment wouldn't last long, though.

And, unfortunately, neither would he.

Drew blinked, trying to keep his eyes open. He'd driven for at least two hours, stopping when he thought he saw lights in the distance, making sure that he didn't turn on his own lights because he hadn't wanted to alert the enemy to his location.

He'd gotten Tina away from those men. He'd done his best by her.

But now he was about to collapse. Too much blood loss. Not enough sleep. He couldn't even remember the last time that he'd slept and, normally, that wouldn't be a problem but—

*The bullet's still in me.* The wound was making him too weak. He had to find a place to hide. A place to rest so that he could get that damn bullet out of him.

Or so Tina could remove it. He had a doc. He was going to use her.

He saw the small ranch, a dot in the distance. Cautiously he drove toward it. The fence was broken, the grass overgrown. No signs of cattle or horses. No sign of anyone.

The windows were boarded up. The roof slumping.

"Are we going there?" Tina asked, her voice barely rising over the rumble of the motorcycle's engine.

He shook his head. Not there. If their pursuers came this way, they'd search the ranch first. But…

Drew drove past the ranch. He kept heading across that overgrown field.

Then he saw the shack. Maybe it had been used as a storage building once or even as a small house for a ranch hand, but time hadn't been kind to the place.

The front window was broken. Two boards had been crisscrossed over the window and nailed in place.

The little structure was nestled behind some trees, so it wouldn't be immediately visible to anyone who came by. And, besides, if their pursuers *did* come this way, they'd check the ranch first.

*And I'll hear them.*

"We're stopping here." He killed the engine.

Tina climbed off the bike, wincing a little, and he followed right after her. They walked the motorcycle to the shack where he hid it in the back and then Drew reached into the saddlebag.

"What's that?" Tina asked as she leaned in close.

"Emergency supplies." Because he believed in being prepared. Would the burner phone work? Only if they could get a signal in the middle of nowhere. It had been hard enough to get a signal at the compound.

Out here…doubtful.

He'd gotten the pack ready cautiously, always knowing that he could need to flee at any moment. Some food, medical supplies—and that burner phone. Everything that a guy on the run could possibly need.

He tucked the bag under his arm and hissed out a breath when his wound throbbed.

"Drew?"

"I'll need your help, Doc." Sure, he'd taken out bullets on his own before, but when he'd stitched them up, he'd done hack jobs on his body. Besides, with the way he was feeling, Drew was afraid he might pass out halfway through the bullet extraction.

He went back to the front of the shack. The door was locked, so he just pulled up his strength and kicked it in.

Inside, dust coated the place. The shack smelled closed-in—but, lucky for them, there weren't any critters.

And the place *had* been a house. Once. He pulled a flashlight from the pack and shone the small ray of light around the interior. An old bed. A table. Some chairs.

He hauled the chairs back against the door and braced them under the now-broken doorknob.

Drew dumped his pack on the wobbly table. He reached inside and pulled out another flashlight. Drew handed it to Tina. "We can't keep the light on for too long. If the folks looking for us come this way, it will alert them."

She nodded.

He lifted the phone.

He realized that Tina was holding her breath.

He hated to break it to her but… "There's no signal here." He'd try to go outside. Walk the perimeter. Maybe he'd find—

His knees buckled. He almost hit the floor. And he almost took Tina down with him.

"Drew!" She braced him against her.

"Sorry, Doc, stood as long…as I could…" He licked his too-dry lips. "Do me a favor?"

"Of course! Anything, I—"

"Dig out the bullet."

She grabbed for the first-aid supplies and helped him to the bed. He fell back and she came tumbling down with him. When he hit the mattress, she fell in close to him. Her mouth was just inches from his. "Want you," he managed to rasp, and maybe he was starting to get a little delirious from the pain and blood loss because he hadn't meant to tell her that. Talk about bad timing. "Got to…stop bleedin' first… Can't die on you…"

"No, *you can't."* Her voice was sharp. She pushed up to stare down at him. But he'd dropped his flashlight when his knees buckled, and he couldn't see her face clearly. Just the darkness.

He wanted her mouth again.

He also wanted to just sleep.

Then he heard fabric ripping. He realized his eyes had sagged closed. He opened them and saw the flash of light. Tina still had her flashlight, and she was shining it on him.

She'd ripped away his shirt.

"How were you even moving?" Tina whispered. "You drove for so long."

Soldiers didn't stop moving. Not until the mission was done. He'd needed to get Tina to safety.

He had.

"Drew!"

He realized that she'd been calling his name. Again and again. He frowned at her.

"I'm going to remove the bullet, and I'll sew you up, but I don't have anything to numb the area. The kit had some alcohol and some antibiotics, but—"

"Do…it," he growled. They'd have to run again, soon. He needed the wound closed by then.

She climbed over him. With them bound, he knew that Tina had to be creative with her movements.

If he hadn't been hurting so much, he would have truly enjoyed having her straddle him.

*Next time.*

She put the flashlight at the top of the old headboard so that it shone down on him. "One hand," she muttered. "I can't believe I have to do this with one hand."

He jiggled their connected wrists. "Use me."

"You're about to pass out on me." She nibbled her lower lip. She'd taken the gloves from the first-aid pack. Put them on. "Don't get an infection. Don't get an infection..."

He didn't think she was talking to him anymore. She seemed to be repeating that mantra to herself.

When she started applying pressure and digging that bullet out, he pulled in a deep breath. He locked his gaze on her face. Focused only on her.

He'd been shot on another mission, just a few months back. He'd been lured into a trap. Hit before he'd had a chance to call for backup. When he'd woken in the hospital, Tina had been there. "You were...worried about me," he said, remembering.

She glanced at him. "Are you staying with me, Drew?"

"Always," he whispered.

"Good. Because I'm not planning to let you go." Her lips curved. She was so gorgeous when she smiled. Did she realize that?

She even had a dimple in her left cheek. A little slash that would peek out every now and then.

The dimple wasn't showing at that moment. Tina had to really smile, had to really laugh, for it to come out. He'd caught her laughing with her friend Sydney once. That was when he'd first seen the dimple.

He'd been lost, staring at her.

"Stitching you up," she said. "Just a little bit longer."

He'd watched her that day, and he'd wanted. But there had been another mission waiting for him. There always was. And, even if there hadn't been, he didn't know how to approach a woman like her.

Wining and dining. Those were tricks that other guys used. He didn't know anything about romance.

He just knew too much about death.

"All done."

Drew glanced down. She'd put a bandage over his wound.

"Thanks, Doc." He owed her. He'd find a way to repay that debt.

"Thanks for getting me out of that place," she whispered back to him. A soft, wet cloth pushed over his skin and smoothed down his chest.

He tensed.

Her hand lightly stroked him. "Easy. It's a bacterial wipe from the kit. I'm just going to clean the blood away."

"Tina…"

Her hand stilled. She looked up at him.

*Focus.* "Don't…leave the house."

She nodded then smiled. One of those real smiles that flashed her dimple.

*Gorgeous.*

"I can't," she told him. Then she was the one to wiggle their cuff. "I can't go any place without you."

The darkness pressed in on him. "Damn straight," Drew heard himself mumble. "That's the way it's going be… here on out…"

And, with Tina's hands on him, with her smile the last sight he'd seen, Drew let the pain finally take him away.

"Where are they?"

Lee Slater froze at the demand. Oh, hell, he hadn't thought the boss would be showing up so soon.

"Did you think I wouldn't hear about this screw-up?" Anton Devast demanded as he stepped forward. Lee could easily hear his footsteps and the *thud, thud, thud* of his cane. "The men here are loyal to me, not you, Lee."

Lee squared his shoulders and spun to face the boss.

The guy in front of him didn't look intimidating. Older, with gray hair at his temples, a slight slump to his shoulders, and the fingers of his right hand curling so tightly around that cane—the guy didn't look like a threat at all.

He was. He was the deadliest man that Lee had ever met. "I've got men tracking them now—"

"You let Bruce Mercer's daughter escape."

Cold. But when he looked into the boss's eyes, that dark blue gaze seemed to burn.

"Sh-she had help." He was stuttering. Because he'd seen the boss in action. The guy was faster than men half his age. "We think… We think an EOD agent was undercover."

"I know. Carl told me."

Carl. Damn it. The guy should have waited for Lee to break the news to the boss.

"Don't be angry at Carl. I *convinced* him to tell me everything as soon as I arrived."

Lee realized that there was blood at the bottom of that cane.

It wasn't just a cane, he knew. A deadly blade could extend from that tip. *Sorry, Carl.*

"An EOD agent, in *my* operation." The boss began to pace around the room. *Thud, thud, thud.* "I should've eliminated Mercer years ago. The same way he tried to eliminate *me.*"

The boss had to use the cane because Bruce Mercer had nearly killed him twenty years before. The boss had almost lost his leg in that explosion.

He had lost his son.

Devast stopped pacing. He lifted the cane and pointed it at Lee. "You have six hours to find them."

Lee nodded quickly. "My men—"

The cane pushed against his throat. The blade extended

just a bit. "No, not your men. *You.* Get out there. Kill the EOD agent and bring that woman back to me."

Lee nodded.

The blade withdrew. The cane dropped.

Lee rushed for the door.

"If you can't bring her back to me, then you'll be the next one to die."

It wasn't an idle threat. Lee grabbed for his backup weapon. He hurried out of the compound and headed toward the helicopter. They hadn't been able to see much at night, but now that day had broken, he was sure he'd be able to track the agent and the woman.

He wasn't dying.

They were.

## Chapter Four

The knife was coming toward her hand. The man with the cold eyes smiled as he prepared to slice off her finger. Tina tried to jerk her hand back, but it was caught on something.

"Easy."

Her eyelids flew open.

Drew stared down at her. "You're safe," he said, the words a low, deep rumble. "You're with me."

Her breath eased out as the nightmare—memory—faded.

They were on the old bed. Still cuffed. And Drew was leaning over her.

A much more aware, focused Drew than she'd seen a few hours ago. Right before he'd passed out on her.

Tina swallowed. Her throat was parched. It must have been at least eight hours since she'd had something to drink, but she figured the dry throat was the least of her worries. Her voice was husky when she asked him, "How are you feeling?"

"More human."

Good. A fast glance showed that there had been no additional bleeding since she'd last checked him. "I don't even know how you stood on your feet for that long. Much less controlled that bike." Anyone else would have been down the instant the bullet hit.

Not Drew. The guy seemed to have a will made of iron.

And now that he wasn't down for the count, she became aware of the fact that they were in a highly intimate situation.

In bed.

His body over hers, his arm curving around her.

Her heart slid into a double-time beat, and that faster pounding wasn't just from fear.

His eyes were on hers. Golden eyes. She'd never seen a man with eyes like his before. They always looked a little wild.

His eyes were so startling because other than his wild stare, he'd always been so controlled in every encounter they'd had back at the EOD offices.

"I—I'm not Mercer's daughter." She wasn't sure why she blurted that out right then. Especially since she'd been staring at him and thinking that his lashes were incredibly long... That his lips were sexy...

That she wanted him to kiss her.

"I know."

He was— Wait. "You do? How?"

He just stared back at her.

*He knows who Mercer's real daughter is.*

But then, so did Tina. But she only knew because Mercer had been so determined to protect one particular agency "asset" a few months ago. On a case that had caused Drew to wind up with more bullet wounds and an emergency trip to the hospital.

The asset had been in that hospital, too, and guarded by other EOD agents. Mercer had wanted to transfer the woman out of that hospital, to move her ASAP. He'd even gone so far as to order the woman drugged.

But, fortunately for the woman in question, EOD Agent Cale Lane had been there. Cale had fallen fast and hard for the asset and he hadn't been about to let anyone threaten her.

Not even the woman's own father.

"You...you worked on her protection detail," Tina said slowly as she put the puzzle pieces together. That was how he knew her identity.

Drew shook his head. "Bruce Mercer doesn't have a daughter." Flat. Hard.

Her brows lifted.

"Bruce Mercer doesn't have a daughter," he said again. "Because if he did, the woman would be a constant target. She'd never be safe."

She understood. Oh, heck, yes, after the past twenty-four hours, Tina definitely understood. "He doesn't have a daughter," Tina repeated. Did Drew think that she wouldn't protect the other woman? She could have sold her out at any time, if that was what she wanted. "I'm not like that," Tina said, suddenly angry because, after everything that had happened, Drew actually thought she'd trade someone else's life for her own. She shoved against him.

But Drew didn't back away. "What's wrong?"

"You think..." Now she was the one gritting out words. "That I would throw someone else at those animals? Knowing that they'd just torture her? Kill her?" She wouldn't stand by and watch an innocent suffer. That wasn't who she was. "I *wouldn't*." She'd had to watch her parents suffer.

Their deaths had almost broken her.

He pinned her hands to the bed. "Calm down."

"You calm down!" Tina snapped at him. "I've been kidnapped, cut, locked up, handcuffed—and I've held it together!" She'd even saved his hide. Where was her thanks?

"I'm not going to betray the EOD, and you should know me better than that."

His hold didn't loosen. "Torture can break anyone, Doc. I've seen seasoned warriors crumble with the right pressure."

"Maybe you should have more faith in me," she told him, the anger snapping in her words. "Now let me go before I damage those stitches!" Because she was fighting mad.

Drew shook his head. "You won't. You won't hurt me. You're a healer. That's what you do." He brought his head close to hers.

Before she could snarl at him, Tina heard a new sound rising in the distance. The unmistakable whir of a helicopter's blades.

She stilled.

"It's okay," Drew told her, but his voice had dropped to a whisper. "They're just doing a sweep. They're not going to see the bike, and they're not going to see us."

She didn't have that confidence. "Maybe they're searching for houses. Places that we could have used for hiding. They could land here—"

He laughed softly at that. "They'll be lucky to land anywhere. A guy named Grayson was the only other pilot there, and when I went up with him once, he could barely hold the bird steady. That's why they were so quick to bring me on board. They needed me."

She still wasn't exactly feeling reassured. Especially because the whir of the helicopter's blades was getting closer and closer—louder and louder.

"Don't think about it," Drew told her. "Think about this."

Then he kissed her. She was still angry at him and scared about the helicopter.

But she had a weakness. One very distinct weakness. She liked kissing him because the man sure knew how to use his mouth.

His tongue licked lightly over her lower lip then it thrust into her mouth. He kissed her slowly, deeply, as if he were savoring her.

She was sure savoring him.

She wanted to wrap her arms around him, wanted to feel the broad expanse of his shoulders, but he still held her hands pinned to the bed.

Other parts of her body could sure feel, though. His arousal pressed against the juncture of her thighs. He'd moved, shifted his weight, so that he was positioned between her legs.

His mouth slipped from hers. He began to kiss his way down her neck. Her breath was coming in fast gasps, and—

"The helicopter is gone," she whispered as she realized an intense quiet had swept over the area.

He kept kissing her neck.

Right. Gone chopper. But focused man. "Drew?"

His head lifted. Those golden eyes seemed to blaze. "I want you."

Her breasts were tight, aching, and when had she started arching her lower body against his? She wasn't normally one to have desire ignite with just a kiss.

But Drew wasn't a normal kind of guy, and the way he made her feel was definitely not normal, too.

Maybe that wasn't bad. It sure didn't feel bad.

It felt incredibly good.

"But our first time together isn't going to be in some shack." That Mississippi drawl slipped in and around his words. "And we won't be covered in blood and grime." He sucked in a deep breath. "I know you deserve better than that." He backed away from her. "But, Doc, to be safe, you better keep that sexy-as-sin mouth away from me, 'cause when I get your lips beneath mine, I lose control."

He'd moved to the edge of the bed. She sat up next to him. Their linked hands were so close. *We might as well be holding hands.* Tina swallowed and tried to steady her breathing. "I didn't think control was a problem for you." Wasn't he supposed to be the cold-blooded agent?

His fingers caught her chin, tilted her head back so that he stared into her eyes. "Don't believe everything you hear." A warning.

"I don't." Tina forced a smile. The tension was thick, and she ached. "If I did, I'd think I was Bruce Mercer's daughter."

His lips twitched again. His fingers fell away from her chin and he glanced toward the cuff on their wrists. His tentative smile faded. "Hell, you're bruising."

She looked down. The skin around the cuff was starting to turn dark. "It's okay." She'd always bruised easily.

He slid from the bed, pulling her with him. "The hell it is. Now that I'm not delirious from pain, I bet I can find something here to get that thing off you."

Tina followed him. Actually bumped into him when he spun back around to face her.

"Don't think it's over," he said, eyes sharp.

What?

His gaze searched hers. "A promise is a promise," he murmured. Then he was heading toward the small table. She followed right beside him, wondering just what he was talking about.

"Making love, Doc. I'm talking about me and you, being naked on clean sheets and enjoying pleasure that lasts all night long."

Oh, man, had she asked her question out loud?

Tina realized that her mouth was hanging open.

"Got it," he said with a satisfied nod.

He had what looked like an old, thin, twisted piece of metal in his hand. It wasn't any bigger than a bobby pin, and when he shoved it into the handcuff lock, Tina knew he hadn't "got" anything.

"That's not going to work," she told him, clearing her throat because she was still thinking about…*being naked on clean sheets and enjoying pleasure that lasts all night long.*

So that was the promise he intended to keep.

"Sure it will work. Trust me. I learned to pick locks early on."

"You did?" *Stop focusing on being naked.* She glanced up at his face. Drew wasn't looking at her. He was concentrating on the lock. "Back before your Delta Force days?"

"Back in my screwed-up-kid days." Said without any emotion. "My dad cut out on my mom and me. She had to work two jobs to cover me and my sisters."

Sisters? Any family information was kept strictly confidential at the EOD.

"Guess you could say that I had a lot of anger about what was going on around me. Growing up dirt poor in Mississippi isn't exactly an easy path. I was a mad kid, in the wrong part of town."

The lock *snicked*. The cuff opened, freeing her wrist. He took care of the cuffs still on him then he lightly stroked the skin of her wrist. "I ran wild back then. Picked up some habits that I shouldn't have."

His touch felt so good on her skin. "I thought you were the one who always played by the rules."

"These days, I try." His gaze dropped to her mouth once more. "But sometimes there are some rules that I have to break."

He was going to kiss her again. She wanted him to—

Drew's head jerked to the left. Toward the broken window. "Hell. Company."

She yanked her hand away from him. "The helicopter left."

"And when Lee spotted the ranch, he might have given orders for his men to search the place." He reached for his pack. "I thought he might do that."

Her body had tensed. "You should have mentioned that 'thought' to me sooner."

He pulled a knife from the pack. "I didn't want you to worry."

Uh, she was worrying plenty right then.

Drew hurried to the window. "I heard their vehicle. The sound of one engine, but I can't see them. Not yet."

She looked around for her own weapon. "Do we make a break for it?" Jump on that motorcycle and ride fast and hard?

He shook his head but didn't glance back at her. "They're searching to push us into a panic. With that chopper in the air, Lee would see us on the bike. No, we don't leave." She saw his grip tighten on the knife. "We hunt."

A HELICOPTER SWOOPED overhead.

Dylan paused beside his truck. He was on the side of the old road, standing next to the apparently broken-down vehicle. The hood was up and his hands were dirty with grease.

"That's the second time that chopper has flown over us," Rachel murmured as she strolled to his side. "Something is definitely going on in this area."

Dylan tilted back his head. "They're searching for—"

He broke off because he'd just spotted another vehicle coming down that long, lonely stretch of Texas road.

There was only one place at the end of that road—the enemy compound.

And the gray pickup that was heading toward him? Those guys were coming from the compound.

The weight of his gun pressed into his lower back. The weapon was hidden beneath his jacket.

They'd planned to get in close to the compound, and this was their first step.

It was also a step that might be ending a little too soon.

The gray truck braked next to him, sending a pile of dust up into the air. Two men were in the vehicle. They were young, both in their early twenties, with dark hair and suspicious eyes.

"You got trouble?" one of the men demanded.

Uh, yeah, didn't it look as though he did?

"The engine overheated," Rachel said easily as she walked toward the truck. "My boyfriend here…he's not so good with cars."

The men's attention fixed a little too quickly on her.

Dylan slammed the hood shut. "She'll be working fine now, *honey*."

"It's not them," one of the men muttered. "Leroy, we need to keep lookin'."

*Not them.* That was exactly the intel Dylan had needed. He headed toward the men, toward Rachel. Dylan made sure his steps were slow and easy. As nonthreatening as possible. He wrapped his arm around her waist and kept his gun concealed. "I think I'm a little lost," he said, giving them a sheepish smile.

One of the men, a fellow with ruddy cheeks and a small gap between his front teeth, eyed Dylan with suspicion. "Where are you headed?" *Leroy.* His buddy had called him Leroy. Dylan filed that name away for later.

"Toward Baker's Ranch," he replied easily. "A dude ranch in—"

"There's no dude ranch this way," he was flatly told. "So get your pretty girl, get in your truck and get the hell out of here."

Rachel stiffened. Her eyes widened as she gave a little gasp. "Is that— Are you threatening us?" Fear slid into her voice. Rachel was a damn fine actress.

"No, 'honey,'" Leroy told her as his gaze slid back toward her. "I'm giving you a warning. There are some dangerous people out in this area. We're hunting them right now."

"Are you a cop?" she whispered. The fear was gone. Now she was sounding all impressed.

Dylan squeezed her hip. *Not too much, Mancini.*

The fellow's chest puffed up. "Something like that," he said.

Wrong. Nothing like that.

"And the guy we're looking for? He's a killer. A cold-blooded, shoot-you-in-the-face killer."

Rachel trembled.

Dylan pulled her closer. "Then we need to get out of here." He gave a quick nod. "Thank you, gentlemen. We appreciate you stopping to try to help us."

As if the guys had even offered help. They'd just ogled Rachel and given their get-out-of-here warning.

But the men had been helpful. *They're looking for Drew.*

There was no point in trying to get inside the compound for an extraction. Not when Drew had to be long gone.

Dylan and Rachel climbed back into their vehicle. Dylan thought he heard one of the guys give a wolf whistle when Rachel's shorts hiked up as she eased into the high seat. Jaw clenching, he cranked the truck and turned it around, heading away from the compound.

"They're watching us," Rachel said as her fingers tapped lightly against her thigh.

He glanced into his rearview mirror. The men were standing in the middle of the road. Just staring after them.

"Now we know why Drew didn't make contact," she added.

He nodded. "Because he's on the run."

"No," Rachel corrected softly, "*they* are. The guy said 'hunting them.' Drew's in the wind, and he took the doctor with him."

That had been Drew's new mission assignment. Protect the woman. And when the blond in that proof-of-life video had gone toward her with that knife, Drew had run out of options.

Dylan's gaze scanned the empty terrain around him. He heard the whir of the helicopter approaching once more. "We have to find Drew before they do."

Because if they didn't, he'd be dead.

"We need to call Sydney," he said, "see if she was able to remotely activate his tracker."

Only…this part of Texas was hell when it came to satellite transmissions and tracking. Cell phones barely worked, and locating Drew's GPS signal could be near impossible.

It was a good thing Dylan liked a challenge.


THREE MEN CLIMBED from the vehicle. A quick check revealed that they were all armed. The HAVOC group always was. "They're coming toward us," Drew said. The men had already checked the ranch and now were splitting apart as they searched the surrounding land.

Tina stood just behind him. She'd grabbed a broken leg from an old wooden chair and was clutching it like a baseball bat. He had no doubt that, if necessary, she'd be ready to swing.

The men had made short work of searching the house. After they'd cleared that place, they should have just gotten in their Ranger and rode the hell out of there.

They hadn't.

Lee must have given orders to thoroughly search the area. So that was exactly what those three bozos were doing.

One suddenly called out, voice excited.

*You don't call out. That alerts your prey.* Amateurs.

But Drew realized they'd seen the shack. He backed away from the window as he planned his attack.

"I want you to stay inside," he told Tina. He didn't want her in the line of fire but he didn't have a whole lot of options. *I'll keep her safe.*

"I can help you," Tina said as her grip on her makeshift bat tightened.

"You will help me." He hated to do this but... "You're going to be my bait."

Her eyes narrowed. "Say that again. I'm going to be your what?"

"When those men get close enough, I want you to call out and beg for help. You're the prize they want. They aren't going to fire on you."

He wouldn't give them the chance to fire.

But he did need them distracted.

"Stay against the wall when you call out. Do *not* let them see your body at all, understand?"

"I understand that I don't like this plan." Her jaw had firmed.

Damn but she was cute. "Think positive. Maybe I'll take 'em out before they even get close enough to hear you." He'd do his best. Drew turned away from her.

Tina's hand wrapped around his arm. "Be careful."

She was worried about him? "Don't worry, Doc, we have unfinished business, right?"

Her fingers jerked back as if he'd burned her.

Ice shouldn't burn.

He left her quickly, ready to eliminate this threat and move on as fast as he could. He exited from the back of the small house. He kept his body positioned close to the old walls. He'd need to circle around for his attack. The problem? There wasn't a lot of cover. So those men had to stay totally focused on what was happening *inside* the house.

Not what was going on outside.

He could hear their footsteps rushing toward them, coming closer and closer with every tense second that passed.

*Now, Doc. I need you now.*

As if on cue… "Help!" Tina shouted. "Please, help me!"

The footsteps moved even faster. Drew crept around the house. He peered around the corner and saw the men at the front door. They weren't even looking his way.

*Mistake.*

He tossed his knife and it sank into one man's side. The guy cried out, and down, down he went.

The other men spun at his cry, but it was too late. Drew grabbed the second guy, applied the right amount of pressure, and he was unconscious seconds later. A fast, hard kick slammed the third man into the side of the wall. His head connected with a thud and he fell with a groan.

"You…*bastard!*"

Technically, he wasn't. Drew spun toward the new threat. The attacker had yanked the knife out of his side and blood dripped down his body as he advanced toward Drew. "I get to kill you," he said, eyes bright. "Lee said you didn't have to come in alive. Not you, just her."

Drew backed up, trying to lead the man away from the house.

"I will *kill*—"

Tina rushed from the house. She swung her chair leg at the man's hand. The knife hit the ground while he howled.

Drew drove his fist into the guy's face.

No more howling.

The guy crumpled on the ground just as nicely as the other two men had.

Tina's breath was coming fast and hard; panting.

Her cheeks were too pale.

Drew frowned at her. "You okay?"

She lifted her hand. "Just give me…" She sucked in more deep breaths. "A minute."

He didn't like the pallor of her cheeks. He reached for her and wrapped his hands around her arms.

Her breathing seemed to slow.

*In. Out. In. Out.*

"You were great," he whispered to her. "I knew you'd be a slugger with that chair leg."

Faint color rose in her cheeks. Her breathing was definitely easier now. After a moment Tina eased away from him and stared down at the unconscious men. "You know I'm going to have to stitch that one up, right?"

"I know we're cuffing them and tying them up." The old bed cover inside would work perfectly once he cut it into strips. He glanced over at the ranch. "Then we're leaving them here and we're taking their ride." Because if Lee saw the Ranger high-tailing it down the road he'd just think his men were continuing their search. The vehicle would be their perfect cover.

Tina smiled. "We're going to make it, aren't we?" Hope lit her face.

He nodded, but Drew didn't actually speak. He'd learned long ago that some lies could taste too bitter on the tongue.

LEE'S HANDS WERE sweating. There was no sign of Mercer's daughter, and if he didn't turn that woman back in to the boss... *I'm dead.*

Anton Devast wasn't exactly big on giving second chances. You messed up once with him and you were dead.

He motioned to Grayson, and the pilot circled the chopper around. The bird jerked in the air, then steadied. Lee hissed out a sharp breath and stared below with grainy eyes. He saw the familiar Ranger heading down the narrow, broken road. Reynolds, Morris and Sanchez. They'd been sent out to the abandoned ranch that he'd spotted. He'd given them orders to radio in if they saw anything suspicious out there.

He squinted as he stared down at them. Their vehicle was moving in the wrong direction. They weren't heading back to the compound. They were going east.

He glanced over at Grayson. "Get Reynolds on the radio." Where the hell was that man going? No one stopped searching, not until Stone was dead and Mercer's daughter was contained.

Lee's life was on the damn line.

*No one stopped.*

TINA STARED AT the small radio cradled in Drew's hand. It had crackled to life a moment before.

"Report!" a man's voice demanded.

Drew glanced over at her. One hand was on the wheel. The other was tightening around the radio. "Clear," he barked. Only that wasn't his normal voice. He'd responded in a voice that was harder, sharper.

"Any—" more crackling "—sign?"

"Not there. Checking to the east. Interference—" Then he slammed the radio into the dashboard.

It splintered into several big chunks.

"Like I said," he muttered, "interference."

She couldn't pull in a deep enough breath. She was trying hard to stay calm, but the panic wanted to rise. Did Drew know? He'd heard her deep, heaving breaths back at the abandoned ranch. Did he realize just how much of a risk she posed to him?

*Breathe. Relax. Picture the air sliding deep into your lungs.*

"You think…they bought that?"

"If the chopper lands in front of us, then they didn't."

The chopper was about fifty yards away and it was—

Leaving.

Tina finally got that deep breath.

"Any signal on the cell?"

She glanced down. "Not yet."

"When we get to Lightning, we'll call in my backup. They can pick up the men we left back at the ranch, and they can get you out of here."

"Lightning?"

"A speck on the map. One of the tiniest towns you've never seen." His lips hitched as he glanced toward her. "As far as rest stops go, it's the only option we have."

"But…but won't those men be looking for us there?"

"Yeah, they will be, and that's why we have to make sure they don't find us." He gave a grim nod. "It's also my backup plan."

"Good to know you have a plan," she said as her fingers curved around the cell phone.

"My team has eyes in that town. They'll be able to back us up. Doc, you may even be on your way to your D.C. apartment by dawn."

That sounded like heaven to her. Going to New Orleans had been such a horrible mistake. And to think, she'd originally believed it would be the perfect, easy assignment. A way to get out of D.C. for a while.

If only she'd known about the danger that awaited in the Big Easy.

But Drew was right. Soon she would be going home once more.

She just had to get through a few more hours of hell first.

DREW HAD BEEN RIGHT. The town of Lightning was so small that if she'd blinked, Tina was sure she would have missed the place. When they drove in, a rumble of thunder followed them.

They passed boarded-up buildings. Two empty gas stations. She saw a diner to the right that looked as though it hadn't been open in years.

"Storms come in here like clockwork," Drew told her as he fired a quick check into the rearview mirror. So far, there had been no sign of company. "Lightning messes up all the electrical equipment in town. Most folks don't like the storms, so they don't stay here long."

Well, that would sure explain the town's name.

He eased off the main road. Well, what passed for the main road anyway. He parked the vehicle behind the diner. "No sense leaving it too close," he said as he took her hand. He'd taken the cowboy hat and a shirt from one of the thugs back at the old ranch. The shirt was a little too small and it stretched over his wide shoulders.

His fingers curled around hers. "Come on. Another storm will be hitting soon."

The sky was pitch-black. More thunder rumbled. She'd

just taken a few steps with Drew when the first raindrops hit her.

Then the dark clouds really opened up. The rain pelted them, hard and fast, as they ran down narrow streets toward an old motel.

The orange Vacancy sign glowed brightly.

It sure was a beautiful sight.

Drew pushed open the motel's office door. A little bell jingled overhead.

No one was inside. No one waited behind the narrow counter. Tina shoved back her wet hair. Her shirt clung to her like a second skin and—

"Good thing you two are here." A woman's voice came from the back corner of the office, making Tina jump. "No one should be out in weather like this."

Tina realized that she'd put her hand over her heart. She was ready to stop having so many scares.

"Hi, ma'am." Drew flashed the woman a smile and tipped back his wet hat. "My wife and I need a room." He pushed some cash across the counter. More than enough cash to cover a room.

And enough to stop any questions?

But the woman—her white hair and the deep lines near her eyes put her in her seventies—was staring at Tina's hand. No. At the dark circle on Tina's wrist.

Frowning, the lady asked, "You okay, miss?"

Tina dropped her hand and forced a big smile. "I'm fine. Just had a little…accident." With a pair of handcuffs.

The woman's gaze slid toward Drew. Now she was looking suspicious. A small name tag on her left breast-pocket indicated the woman's name was Sarah.

"Maverick," he said softly.

And, just like that, the woman's face cleared of all emotion. She handed Drew a room key. "Room six. Last one on the end." She turned around and headed into the back room.

Tina blinked. What was that about?

Drew reached for Tina's hand. His fingers stroked her wrist. "We'll get some ice for that."

A bruised wrist wasn't especially high on her list of worries right then.

They had to run back into the rain to get to their room. But, less than three blessed minutes later, they were inside room number six. The place was small but clean, so wonderfully clean, and dry.

Lightning flashed outside the window. Thunder rumbled and the window glass trembled.

Drew locked the door behind her.

Tina wrapped her hands around her stomach. "There's a phone on the nightstand." A landline. She'd never been so happy to see one of those before. "Are you going to call Mercer now?"

"I don't need to." He tossed away his hat and wiped his hand over his hair. The hat hadn't exactly kept his dark hair dry. Droplets of water fell around him. "Sarah knows the score. She's already made contact with the base group."

"Sarah?" Her eyes widened. "That sweet old lady at the desk—"

"She's ex-EOD. She recognized my code word. She'll make sure that word spreads fast that we're here. My team will come for us."

That was good. That put her one step closer to ending this nightmare. It also meant that she was one step closer to leaving Drew.

*Not so good.*

He turned toward the window. "Why don't you go shower off? You'll feel more human after—"

"After I wash the blood and dirt away?" Tina finished.

Yes, she would. But she felt as though there was more she should say to him. If the cavalry was coming in to swoop her away at any minute, there *had* to be more she told him. So she started with the basics. "Thank you."

He turned toward her.

Another bolt of lightning flashed, illuminating the area just beyond the window.

The thunder rumbled a moment later.

"You blew your cover to save me." No, more than that. Tina's gaze held his. "You risked your life." He'd taken a bullet for her. How was she supposed to repay that kind of sacrifice?

He took a step toward her.

"I didn't ask who those men were." Because she knew the way the system worked. Need-to-know info.

She wasn't an agent. That meant, according to Mercer, the less she knew, the better. Even if her life had been put on the line.

"You're better off not knowing," Drew said, sounding way too much like Mercer for her peace of mind right then. His jaw tightened. "They're some of the most dangerous SOBs that I've crossed."

"You could have died saving me."

He took another slow, gliding step toward her. Then one more. She tilted her head back. Trembled as the rain water began to dry on her skin.

"Doc, I wasn't leaving you behind." His eyes raked her. "And I wasn't going to let them hurt you anymore. Carl wasn't using that knife on you."

She was so out of her league. Not just in the middle of this blood fest, but with Drew.

The guys she dated were nice, safe. They didn't know how to take down enemies in hand-to-hand combat. They didn't know how to pick the locks on handcuffs.

And those men didn't make her feel the way Drew did.

When the cavalry did come through that door, she'd leave the motel. Drew would go back to his missions, and she'd see him when he came in for his checkups at the EOD.

They'd go back to business as usual.

She didn't want that.

What she wanted—was him.

Unfortunately she was a sopping-wet mess at that moment. No doubt, she appeared like a drowned rat.

A seduction routine wasn't going to work right then.

Tina nodded and tried to pull herself together again. "I'm glad you were the agent who was there, Drew." Then she swept around him before she did something crazy— such as throw her arms around the guy and hold on tight.

Or point out the fact that the bed behind them appeared very, very clean.

She opened the bathroom door and rushed gratefully inside. Before she shut the door, she heard him mutter, "I'm glad, too, Doc."


THEY'D ESCAPED. Not just escaped, but seemingly *vanished*. Lee stormed away from the helicopter. He had to tell the boss that the search hadn't turned up the missing woman. This wasn't the way he wanted things to go down.

He hurried by the base's parking area. More of the search teams had come back in, but they'd turned up nothing.

"You didn't find them." *Thud. Thud. Thud.*

Lee froze. The boss wasn't inside the compound. He was right there waiting to attack. "I'm going back out. They must have gotten to a town. Got shelter. We'll get them—"

*Thud. Thud.* "No, if they made it to a town, then the

agent will be calling for backup. He'll be bringing in men to take the woman away."

"Boss, look—"

His words were interrupted by the loud banging of a horn. "What the hell?" Lee said as he turned toward the sound.

He recognized the pickup heading toward him. Leroy and Guan were coming in hell-fast, but three men were hanging on to the back of their pickup.

Reynolds? What the hell was he doing with Leroy? Reynolds had radioed that he was heading east to search.

Lee ran toward the truck. Reynolds was trying to jump off the side of the vehicle's bed. He was missing his shirt and dried blood coated his skin.

"Ambushed us…" Reynolds yanked up his hand—a hand that was connected by a handcuff to Adam Morris. "SOB took our ride and headed out!"

Lee's heart raced faster. "East." He snarled that one word.

"We found 'em," Guan was saying, "when we went over to do a backup sweep at that abandoned ranch. They were tied up in some shack."

"Head east!" Lee bellowed. Because that was where the Ranger had been going. East. There was only one safe spot within a two-hundred-mile radius that way. "Lightning."

They'd gone to that old town.

Now he knew exactly where his prey was hiding.

*Thud. Thud.*

He whirled around. "Don't worry," Lee said quickly to Devast. "I've got them." *My six hours aren't up.*

He'd blow up that whole town if he had to, but he'd get that agent.

*Or I'll die trying.* Because the look in his boss's eyes

clearly said that if he came back empty-handed, death would be waiting on him.

ANTON DEVAST WATCHED Lee Slater rush away. Slater was proving to be a disappointment to him.

When he was disappointed, it meant it was time for people to die.

If Slater couldn't catch the EOD agent and the missing woman, Anton would just have to find someone else to get the job done.

He smiled. Mercer had infiltrated Devast's group. *Thought you were clever, didn't you, old friend?*

It was Anton's turn now. And he'd use one of Mercer's men against him.

In their business, loyalties were bought and traded every single day. You just had to know the right price to offer.

With the right price, you could buy anything.

You could even buy your way into the EOD.

## Chapter Five

The storm wasn't letting up. In fact, the rain pelted down even harder as Drew gazed out the window. His team was coming. He hadn't used the landline to call them. Even in a place that was supposed to be secure… Well, he knew better than to take risks.

Risks would get a man killed.

Sarah had instantly recognized his code word. She would have gone into the back and made contact through a secure system. As a backup—because Drew always believed in backups—he had used his burner phone to check in with Dylan. Now that they were in the town, he'd managed to get a signal strong enough to make the call. His friend and team leader had given him an ETA of less than thirty minutes.

Thirty minutes, and then Tina would be gone.

*That's not enough time with her.*

The bathroom door opened with a soft creak. He turned to look at her. Steam drifted lightly from the small bathroom.

A loud crack of lightning seemed to explode outside the motel room.

The room—the whole motel from the look of things— was immediately plunged into darkness.

"Drew?"

Even in the dark, he saw her form easily. Drew had always been gifted with excellent night vision. He stalked toward her. "Told you," he said softly, "the storms come in and cause chaos in the town." The lights might come back on in a few minutes or it could be a few hours before the electricity was restored. *She'll be long gone by then.*

His fingers lifted and curled around her shoulder. Her *bare* shoulder. Her skin was like hot silk beneath his callused fingers.

In that one moment, before the lights had flashed off, he'd seen her standing in that doorway. She'd just been wearing a towel.

Desire, need for her, pulsed beneath his skin. He'd be sent back into the field. If not on this case, then out on another one. How long would it be before he saw her again?

Now that she was compromised, now that the crazies with HAVOC mistakenly thought that she was Mercer's daughter, what would happen to her? She wouldn't be able to go back to her old life.

Not with that threat hanging over her.

*I'll eliminate that threat.*

"My clothes had blood on them," she whispered. "I just… I hated to put them right back on, but I didn't have anything else to wear."

He motioned toward the bed. It was just a big, dark shadow. She probably didn't even see his hand moving. "Sarah brought you some jeans and a fresh shirt."

She didn't move to get those clothes.

"I have a confession," Tina told him softly. "I've… watched you." Her voice was husky in the dark. "At the EOD offices."

He'd watched her plenty, too.

Intrigued now, he waited.

"I know I'm not your usual type of…of date—"

"Oh?" He was even more curious now. "You think I don't go for the smart and sexy women?" Because Tina was most definitely his type. His sleepless nights could attest to that.

"You live on the edge. You love danger and action. And I hide in the background."

No, she *tried* to hide in the background. She failed at that job. A woman like her could never just disappear.

"I don't want to hide from you," Tina told him. Her hands rose and her fingers settled around his shoulders. She was so small, seemingly fragile in front of him. "I want to be with you."

He stiffened as desire sharpened within him. "You should be very careful what you say." Especially to a man like him. A man who'd lived for too long wanting things that he couldn't have.

One of those things was right in front of him.

"It's just us," she said, and her voice was pure temptation. "No gunshots. Not even any lights. Just us. Alone in the dark." She rose onto her tiptoes.

His fingers locked around her waist. "I warned you before about what would happen if I kissed you again." *Naked. Pleasure...*

"I don't want a warning. I told you, I just want you." Then she kissed him.

The need, the raw lust that he felt for her, shot through him and electrified his whole body. Her kiss was tentative, and he needed more than that. So much more. He lifted her into his arms, holding her easily despite his wound.

Tina was right. They were alone. He'd been imaging her spread out in that big bed and, with the lights off, with the dark around them...

*I'll make her mine.*

And when she was taken away from him, Tina would remember what they'd shared.

Drew knew he'd never forget.

Her lips were open and soft beneath his. His tongue slipped into her mouth, and she arched against him. Two steps and he was at the foot of the bed. His knees bumped into the mattress. He lowered her onto the covers, but he couldn't make his hands let her go.

There was too much silken skin to touch and explore. The towel had come loose, and it barely covered her breasts. His fingers eased up her arms. Trailed over her shoulders then moved down her sensual curves.

He got that towel out of the way, yanked it aside.

His mouth followed the path of his hands. Drew kissed her shoulders. He inhaled her sweet scent—still strawberries. Even after everything she'd been through.

Her breasts thrust toward him.

Thunder rumbled once more.

He bent his head over her breast. Put his mouth on one tight nipple. She arched toward him and her fingers sank into his hair.

He liked the sounds she made when he touched her. But even more, he liked the way she was becoming wild for him.

His arousal strained against the fly of his jeans. He wanted to be flesh to flesh with her, to be as close as he could possibly get.

His hand slid down over the curve of her stomach. Her hips were still lifting toward him. His fingers eased between her legs.

"Drew?"

She was warm and responsive and so amazing to touch. He had to explore her. Every single inch.

The fantasy between them would end soon. But he'd take these moments. He'd hold them tight.

*And she won't forget me.*

He stroked her, caressed her and made sure that her desire wound tighter and tighter with every press of his fingers. Her body trembled against his. Her breath came faster.

He found the center of her need. Right there. Right—

A cry of pleasure spilled from her lips. She held him tighter as she shuddered against him.

Hell, yes. And that was just the beginning.

He reached for the snap of his jeans.

And heard footsteps outside the motel room.

Drew tensed.

"Drew—"

He put his mouth on hers and kissed her deeply once more. He could taste her pleasure.

His own body ached. He wanted to drive into her more than he wanted his next breath.

But the footsteps were coming ever closer.

"Outside," he whispered against her lips.

When she stiffened, he knew she understood. Their visitors could be his backup, or it could be the men from HAVOC.

Though it hurt him—*so close*—Drew slid off the bed. He handed Tina the clothes that Sarah had brought for her.

She dressed quickly.

He grabbed the gun Sarah had brought to him.

Drew eased toward the door. Tina's heady scent still filled his nose. He could still taste her.

But their moment of reprieve was at an end. *Too soon.*

He pulled back the curtains, just a tiny space, and gazed outside. Darkness.

That was all right.

The darkness wouldn't last forever.

Lightning flashed.

He saw the outline of two bodies.

A man and a woman. No weapons in their hands, but he could see the holsters for their guns.

He studied the two figures in that instant of light.

And the tension eased from his shoulders.

Drew opened the door. "As always," he said to Dylan Foxx and Rachel Mancini, "your timing is hell."

Dylan grinned at him. "Good to see you, too—"

Thunder blasted.

*The hell that was thunder!*

Wood splintered from the top of the door as Dylan and Rachel leaped inside the motel room.

Drew knew they'd also recognized that sound for exactly what it was—gunfire.

Drew shoved the door closed even as more bullets came flying through the air. "Anyone hit?" he demanded.

"Just a graze," Rachel panted. "What a...*jerk.*"

The glass in the window shattered. The shots were coming so quickly that Dylan knew they were looking at more than one shooter.

"You were followed," Drew said as he immediately took up a fighting stance. His gaze swept the room. Tina had ducked behind the bed. Good. She was safe.

Now to eliminate this threat.

"Bull," Dylan snapped. "We know how to cover our trail."

"Looks like you didn't cover it well enough this time." Drew hated being pinned in that motel room. The only way out would be through some back windows, and there might be men out there, waiting to take a shot at them.

"Let's just hope all of HAVOC isn't out there," Rachel

said as she checked her gun. "'Cause this could be one very long fight."

A bullet ripped through the wood on the motel room door. "Tina!" Drew cried out as worry snaked through him. Innocents got hurt too easily in firefights. "Make sure you stay down." Because when he rushed outside, the bullets would start coming twice as hard and twice as fast.

But there wasn't a choice for Drew.

They weren't going to stay trapped.

Dylan slanted a glance at him. They'd worked together for so long, the guy would know exactly what Drew was planning. "You sure about this?"

He rolled the tension from his shoulders. He'd gone from touching heaven to facing hell in five short minutes. "Just give me cover."

Rachel eased closer to the window. She took aim.

Dylan took a position right next to her. They opened fire.

And Drew rushed out the front door.

DREW LANCASTER was *insane*.

The man had just run out into a hail of bullets. He *had* to be insane.

The thunder was pretty much continuous around Tina then. She could hear the bullets thudding into the walls. Hear the shattering of glass and—wow—the bedside lamp had just blasted into about a hundred small pieces.

*You'd better be alive, Drew. Do not get yourself shot.*

Tina stayed low. She didn't have a weapon to use in this battle. She also couldn't let herself become any kind of handicap to the agents. Her heart was racing, her hands shaking, but she breathed in and out, in and—

Silence.

Tina started to lift her head.

"I count two men down." That was Dylan Foxx's voice. Deep, rumbling, no accent at all. She'd seen Dylan plenty of times at the EOD office.

"There were at least four shooters," Rachel Mancini said. Her voice was softer, and Tina had to strain to hear it. Usually, if Rachel was around, Dylan wasn't far away. They always worked missions together.

Rachel and Dylan were still safe but...

*Where is Drew?*

"I'm going out," Dylan said.

Great. Now two of them were rushing into enemy fire.

*I can help.* She crawled forward. Keeping her head down was a definite priority, but so was making certain that Drew was safe. She grabbed Dylan's leg. He jerked toward her. "Give me a gun," she said, gazing up at him and hoping that he didn't notice her body was shaking. "And I'll help cover you."

He hesitated.

Fine. She yanked up his jeans, revealing his ankle holster. The guy always carried his backup. "I'll just take this one," she told him.

He blinked.

There was still no more gunfire. The silence out there was scaring her as much as the bullets. "Go find Drew."

Dylan nodded. His gaze darted toward Rachel.

The dark-haired agent gave an almost imperceptible nod.

Then Dylan was easing open the motel-room door. He slid into the night.

Tina's knees brushed across the broken shards of glass from the window. The rain still poured from the sky, and the darkness seemed so complete outside. The brief flashes of lightning lit up the scene, and every time it flashed, she strained to see—

"He's got a gun!" The figure lurched up from the darkness and aimed right at the motel room.

Rachel fired.

Tina did, too. The bullets hit the would-be shooter, and the man stumbled back.

Her heart slammed into her ribs. The frantic beating was so powerful that she ached.

"Clear!" That sharp voice calling out—it was Drew's.

She didn't release her death grip on the gun.

"Four men down," Drew shouted. "I need the doc out here!"

He was hurt. In an instant Tina was on her feet. She grabbed for the doorknob.

"Wait—" Rachel began.

No, Drew needed her. There was no waiting.

She ran from the room. Another flash of lightning illuminated Drew. He was on the ground. She could smell blood. "Drew?" Tina reached for him.

He turned toward her. Rain water dripped down his face. "I'm okay, Doc." He pointed to the man on the ground. "He isn't."

Another flash of lightning showed her the face of the man who'd held her hostage. Drew had called him Lee. *Lee.* The man who'd used his phone to record her video proof of life.

The guy who'd callously ordered that her finger be cut off.

"The others are dead," Drew said as the rain hit them. "Lee is the only one left alive out here."

Lee was choking on his own blood. Bullet wounds lined his chest. His eyes were wide and stark, terrified.

This was the man who'd wanted to use her. To hurt her.

Tina sank to her knees. *I need tools.* "I have to get the

bullets out." *Have to stop the blood. Have to try to stabilize him. His blood pressure will be dropping. And—*

She heard the wheeze coming from his lungs. When she leaned forward and looked at his mouth, she could see the small mist of blood shoving past his lips.

"He's got a bullet in his lung." She grabbed Lee's shirt and ripped it apart. The rain kept pelting down on her. She needed to get him inside and—

There were two holes in his chest. One bullet had hit his lung. One had driven in close to his heart. Too close.

A hard hand closed around her wrist, jerking on the bruised skin.

"Don't even think about it, Lee," Drew snarled in the same instant.

Lee had a tight hold on her. He was trying to sit up.

The man should have realized that he didn't have strength to waste fighting her. He should also have realized—

Drew had his gun locked on the man.

"You don't need that," Tina said softly, sadly. Because unless she could get serious help to the injured man within the next few moments…

*He'll be gone. He won't be able to hurt anyone.*

"M-Mercer's…daughter…" The words were forced from Lee's throat. Blood dripped from his lips.

"You need to take it easy," she told him. No one's last moments should be filled with agony.

But Lee smiled at her. "Y-you're gonna die…"

*No, you are. In just a few moments.* Had she done this? Had her shot hit him?

She'd seen brutal death just like this before. Her father had been hit in the chest with a bullet. Her mother had been hit in the heart.

The wrong place. The wrong time.

They'd gone into the local bank, so happy. They'd planned to close out Tina's savings account right before she went to college.

They'd walked into death.

The bank robbers hadn't cared about her family. The robbers had just panicked when Tina began having one of her attacks.

They'd killed her mother instantly.

Her father—it had taken him longer to die. His lungs had slowly filled with blood.

It wasn't going to take Lee as long to die. Not with that shot so close to his heart. Had it nicked the heart? A valve? She glanced over at Drew. "His heart—"

"I can...feel it..." Lee muttered. "Know...what's comin'..."

Her gaze slid to him once more. Under the flash of lightning, Lee didn't look scared. He looked furious.

"Think you're...winnin'...agent..." Lee's lips twisted into a gruesome smile. "But he's not...done..."

Drew pulled Tina away from the dying man. "Who's not done?"

Footsteps rushed toward them. Dylan and Rachel.

"We checked the rest of the perimeter," Dylan said as he closed in. "We're clear."

The rain eased up, dripping lightly over them instead of pelting down.

The thunder had stopped.

No more thunder. No more gunshots.

"Devast...wants...her..." Lee's voice was a harsh rasp. "Won't...stop...until he gets...*her*..."

"Devast won't touch her," Drew swore. "He's out at the compound now, isn't he? Your boss? I'm going after him. I'm going to—"

"Devast...won't stop—"

A sharp breath slipped from Lee.

"Anton Devast?" Drew demanded as he bent over Lee. "I know how many lives he's taken. He won't—"

Tina put her hand on his shoulder. "He's gone." She'd heard that last, hard wheeze that had stilled in Lee's throat.

"Damn it!" Drew surged back to his feet.

Tina leaned over the body. She felt for his pulse, just to be certain, but with the massive trauma to his chest…

*Gone.*

She shivered as the raindrops trailed down her body. The past and the present both slid through her mind.

*You can't save them.* The cops on scene had told her that over and over again as she'd clung desperately to her parents.

Tina glanced at her hands. Even in the dark, she could see the blood.

"Get her inside," Drew said to Rachel as his fingers closed around Tina's shoulders. "Dylan and I will handle the cleanup."

Cleanup. Because there were other bodies out there. Wait, maybe… "Are you sure they're all dead? Maybe some of them are still alive."

Drew shook his head.

She turned toward the motel room. The place looked totally trashed from the outside. Sarah was there, and Tina saw her edging toward them cautiously.

The chill of death seemed to permeate the air. Tina squared her shoulders. "I'm ready to go home now." It was time to leave Drew's bloody world behind.

Time to leave…him.

*THUD. THUD. THUD.*

Anton Devast slowly walked toward the waiting helicopter. The compound was being evacuated. The few men left were scattering.

This base wouldn't be operational—not when the EOD agents swarmed. And they would swarm.

*One of those bastards was here.*

Mercer was smart, and his agents were smart. It had only been a matter of time until they'd infiltrated his network.

But it didn't matter. He'd found Mercer's weakness. *Tina Jamison.* He had pictures of the woman. Videos.

She wasn't escaping from him.

Lee hadn't checked in. That meant the man was either dead or running. If he had tried to flee, well, Lee would be dead in hours.

Anton stared into the waning night. He'd waited years for his vengeance. He'd bided his time, made powerful connections and planned so carefully.

He didn't have many days left on this earth. The cancer that had ravaged him before was coming back. Before he died, he had to finish his job.

It wasn't about destroying the U.S. government. Wasn't even about taking down the EOD and the agents who thought it was their job to stick their noses into private affairs.

It was about Bruce Mercer.

About making the man suffer.

Bruce hadn't agreed to trade his life for his daughter's. That had been his mistake. He'd had an option. A chance.

There would be no more chances.

It wasn't about a trade anymore.

It was about a life.

One life for another.

*Vengeance.*

Mercer would understand his pain now. He'd feel the

same agony that Anton had experienced. But there would be no relief from that pain. There was *never* any relief.

"Burn the place to the ground," he ordered as he left the ranch.

*Thud. Thud.*

The base had already been set to ignite. The first explosion detonated and the flames burst into the air. The scent of fire drifted on the wind. He didn't look back at the flames.

He was too busy looking ahead—and planning for Tina Jamison's death.

## Chapter Six

Tina wasn't looking at him. She hadn't looked Drew directly in the eyes since Lee Slater's death.

They were at the airport; a small strip that was used just for government operations. A plane waited behind Tina.

This was the moment he was supposed to let her go. *Why won't she look me in the eyes?*

"Thank you," Tina said. Her voice didn't sound right. Too stilted. Too polite. "I can't ever repay what you did for me."

He didn't care that they had an audience. Drew took her hand in his. Her skin was incredibly soft—he'd never get used to that silken feel beneath his rough fingers. "I want you to watch your back."

Her eyelashes flickered. "Rachel is going to D.C. with me. I'll be perfectly—"

"You won't be safe, not until we have Anton Devast in custody." She'd heard the name already, when he'd been trying to force a last-ditch confession from Lee, so he wasn't breaking any clearance by telling her. Hell, after all she'd been through, the woman *deserved* to know who was after her.

He didn't care about Mercer's rules right then. Not with her life on the line.

Tina glanced at him. Wet her lips. "Do I want to know… the things that he's done?"

No. Drew didn't even want to know. The tortures. The murders. Anton's network stretched halfway across the world. Getting to the man, eliminating him, had been a goal of the EOD for years.

But Anton Devast was a hard man to kill. Getting close to him was practically impossible.

*I was almost there. One more day. I would have been up close and personal with the man.*

But Tina had come first. His hold tightened on her. "He's not just going to walk away from you. He's convinced that you're Mercer's daughter. Stay alert."

"And you stay alive." She gave him a sad smile. One that made his chest ache. "I've grown rather fond of you, Agent Lancaster. I know there's more than just ice running through your veins."

For her, there was fire.

She looked back at the plane that waited. The pilot stood outside, his hands on his hips.

"We need to go, miss!"

Drew just didn't want to let her go.

*It's not about what I want.*

If he had his way, he'd be the one sticking to her like glue. But Mercer's orders had come down. This flight was Tina's safe passage back to D.C.

Drew's job wasn't finished. He was to head back to the Devast base. He was supposed to start picking up the pieces of this mission and track the HAVOC ringleader once more.

What he wanted… He wanted to kiss Tina. To taste her again.

*Not here.*

Drew cleared his throat. "Remember what I promised you we'd have?"

*Naked, tangled together.*

Her pupils widened. Her lips parted.

"I keep my promises."

He let her hand go.

Tina stared up at him. Finally, *finally,* she was looking deeply into his eyes. "You'd better."

She turned away. She and Rachel began heading toward the plane.

Watching someone walk away had never been harder.

Bruce Mercer drummed his fingers on his desk. Tina Jamison was safe. She was on her way back to him.

Dragging her into this mess had been a mistake. A miscalculation. He didn't make those often, but when he did...

The phone vibrated on his desk. Not the confidential office phone.

His personal phone.

Only a handful of people knew his number. He picked it up instantly, thinking it was his daughter, Cassidy.

*Unknown number.*

Tension tightened his body as he read the message on the phone's screen. He answered the call with a curt, "Hello?" He didn't identify himself. Never would.

"Hello, old friend." That voice—that familiar voice—stopped time for him.

Twenty years... It had been twenty years since he'd last heard from Anton Devast.

How had the SOB gotten his private number?

"You always underestimated me," Anton murmured. "That was such a shame."

Mercer didn't speak. He wouldn't. There was no sense giving the man any more information than Devast already possessed. And for Devast to get his private line...

*He has far more intel and connections than I realized.*

"I know where your daughter is…"

No, the guy didn't. He didn't even know who Mercer's real daughter was.

*My Cassidy is on her honeymoon now. With one of my best agents at her side. A man who'd die for her in an instant. She's safe, and you can't touch her.*

"Your girl is flying through the sky. Safe?" Anton laughed. "No. She's not safe. You know what I do best."

Destroy. Terrorize.

"There won't be anything left of her." More laughter. "You should have agreed to the trade. Then you would be the one dying and she'd still have a shot at life."

*Click.*

Sweat slickened Mercer's temple. That call could have been a hoax. A trick to mess with his head. To cause panic and force him to make a mistake.

Except…

*Anton Devast doesn't make threats.*

The bastard delivered promises.

In the next second Mercer was dialing fast and frantically on his phone, calling the one agent who should be able to help him.

*Don't be too late. Don't be…*

THE PHONE IN Drew's pocket vibrated. Frowning, he yanked it up to his ear. Dylan had just given him the replacement phone an hour ago. There weren't many folks who should be trying to reach him then.

He began, "Hel—"

"*Get to Tina Jamison.*" Bruce Mercer's voice barked the order.

Drew's head snapped up. Tina was heading onto the plane.

Drew started running.

"Get to her, Lancaster. Secure her. You saved her before and you damn well better save her now—"

"Tina!" Drew bellowed.

Tina turned toward him. Her head tilted, the sunlight glinting off her dark hair and the replacement glasses that she'd been given.

Rachel was just steps behind her. Rachel frowned at him. "What's happening?"

Rachel had a phone. Rachel was the one who'd been assigned guard duty to Tina. Why hadn't Mercer called her?

"Drew? What's wrong?" Tina took a few steps away from the plane.

The pilot had vanished. Was he inside? Getting ready for takeoff?

Tina shook her head. "I don't understand—"

Mercer was shouting something in his ear.

He needed to get to Tina.

He needed to—

The plane exploded.

BRUCE MERCER STARED at the phone in his hand. He'd heard an explosion, then…nothing.

"I can't get anyone to check in at the scene."

He looked up at his assistant's voice. Judith Rogers stood in the doorway, her eyes wide and worried.

"Keep trying. Someone is there." *Someone has to be.* He'd called Drew because he trusted the man to protect Tina. Bruce was good at observing people, and he'd watched Lancaster and the doctor.

*Drew will keep her safe.*

Judith didn't look reassured. "Tina…?"

"She's fine." This was *his* fault. But he'd fix it. "Drew Lancaster was on scene. I gave him orders to protect her."

Drew had always followed mission orders. The guy did his job and he didn't hesitate. "Drew has her."

But his palms were sweating.

"I hope you're right." Judith turned away. Judith knew most of his secrets. "Because if you're not, I'm not sure how you'll sleep tonight."

Yes, she knew his secrets and his sins.


"Tina!"

Drew was yelling her name again.

He seemed to do that a lot lately.

Her eyes cracked open. Drew was hunched over her. His face was haggard. And— "Do I smell smoke?"

He yanked her into his arms and nearly squeezed the breath from her.

With that crushing embrace, memories flooded back through her mind. She'd been about to board the plane. She hated small airplanes like that one, but she'd been determined to suck up her fear. Then Drew had called out to her.

And the world had exploded.

Smoke thickened the air around her. Tina pulled away from Drew and glanced over her shoulder. The plane was still burning out on the tarmac. "Rachel?" Fear cracked the word.

"She's okay. Dylan has her." Drew rose, pulling Tina to her feet, too. He kept a steady hand on her. "I thought I was going to be too late."

She couldn't take her eyes off the plane. Had the pilot gotten out in time? The flames were wild, burning so high and bright.

Sirens wailed behind her.

"A bomb, Devast's weapon of choice." Drew's words

vibrated with fury. "But how did he get close enough to plant it with so many agents here?"

"The pilot…" She licked her lips, tasted fire and ash. "He's dead?"

"Pierce didn't come out of the plane," Drew said grimly.

Her heart squeezed in her chest.

Another minute and she would have been on that plane, too. She wouldn't have come out.

Dark smoke swirled in the air around her. She tried to suck in air.

*Breathe in. Breathe out.*

But her normal routine for calming an attack wasn't working.

A fist had her heart. Her lungs were burning. Clogged. Her eyes watered as she tried to pull in air. The muscles of her neck and chest were tightening. Clenching.

"Tina? Tina, what's wrong?"

Her streaming eyes found his. "At-tack…" She needed her medicine. The inhaler that would help her.

But there was no inhaler there. Not in the middle of that burning tarmac. No medicine. No help. And she remembered another time. Another place.

*At the bank…she'd struggled to breathe. Her lungs burned. Her chest ached. The men with guns were shouting and fear clawed through her. Her father and mother had rushed to her because they'd known what was happening. Her father had reached into his jacket, grabbing for the inhaler he always carried, ever since her first attack had put her in the hospital at three years old. When he'd reached for that inhaler, one of the masked robbers yelled—then shot her father.*

Her breath wheezed out. The smoke was so thick and dark. The smoke surrounded her. She couldn't get air in—

"I need help!" Drew yelled. He was rubbing her back. "Baby, breathe for me. Nice and slow, okay?"

Didn't it appear as if she was trying?

"Look at me."

Her gaze flew to his once more.

"Breathe with me," he said. "In and out."

It wasn't that easy. It wasn't some mind-over-matter thing right then. She was wheezing, and soon—soon she wouldn't even be able to do that. She could barely pull in any air at all.

Tina knew the power of a severe attack when it struck her.

*The pilot is dead. I was nearly on that plane. People are dying—because of me.*

*Blood. Death. Everywhere.*

"Tina. Tina, focus on me."

She wanted to, but dark spots were dancing in front of her eyes. Her body trembled.

He caught her before she could fall. He scooped her into his arms and started running toward the sounds of those sirens. "I need a medic, now!"

The smoke was too heavy in the air. Even when she did manage to pull in a breath, it was coated in smoke.

"Her lips are blue, damn it. Help me!"

She saw the swirl of flashing lights. Finally something other than the darkness of the smoke. The EMTs reached for her and pulled her away from Drew.

She didn't want to leave him. Her hand flew out, caught his.

"Don't worry, Doc." His voice was steady and strong. "I'm not going anywhere."

The EMTs loaded her in an ambulance; a breathing mask was slid over her face.

Drew was right beside her.

The ambulance roared away as the team got to work on her.

SHE FELT AS if she'd been hit by a truck. Tina sat on the edge of the narrow hospital bed, clad in a thin, paper gown, and she let her breath whisper slowly past her lips.

*At least I'm still alive.*

They'd given her medication to stabilize her breathing. The medication had stopped what might have just been the worst attack of her life.

She'd been helpless. A prisoner, beaten by her own body. And he'd seen her. Drew had been there every moment. Now he knew just how weak she truly was.

The door opened. She didn't glance up. She'd been told by Dylan that guards had been posted outside her room. It seemed that she couldn't go anywhere without a guard now.

Because she was targeted for death.

"Why didn't you tell me?"

She'd known that it was him, of course. Whenever Drew was in the room, her body responded with an awareness that was almost frightening.

Tina wasn't sure that she liked being that tuned to another person.

His fingers brushed over her arm. "Doc?"

She forced her shoulders to straighten. "There wasn't anything you could do while we were on the run. It wasn't like you were going to have asthma medication in your back pocket—or even in your handy motorcycle saddlebag."

She'd been managing to keep the asthma in check. She'd handled the motorcycle ride just fine. Tina had thought she could keep controlling the asthma. Until the plane had exploded. Until the smoke had choked her. Until— "Has Pierce been recovered?"

Drew shook his head. "There's…not going to be much left to recover."

Right. Her eyes closed for an instant. That last little bit of hope left her.

"Tina?"

Her eyes opened. "How did Devast know I was getting on that plane?" The EOD had made arrangements for her flight out of Texas. She should have been safe.

"I slipped into his network," Drew said quietly, his gaze watchful on her face. "And it looks like he managed to slip someone into ours."

Her heart seemed to ache with each beat. From past experience, she knew the soreness would last for a while. "You're saying we have some kind of double agent in the EOD?"

He nodded. "It looks that way."

"Who?"

"That's what we have to find out. And we *will* find out."

"Before," she demanded because it was too much, "or after I'm dead?"

His hands rose and curled around her shoulders. "I'm not letting you die."

Didn't he get it? "You saw me." She pressed her lips together so they wouldn't tremble. Shame burned in her, but she pushed past it. "When an attack hits me, there is nothing I can do. I'm too vulnerable. If there's a double agent in the EOD, he can find out my secret." *If he doesn't already know.* "I'm easy to kill." The paper gown scraped across her knees as she shifted uncomfortably. "Too easy."

"I'm not letting you die," he said again, voice rougher.

"You can't save everyone, you know." That was a lesson she'd been taught long ago. Sometimes you couldn't even save the ones who mattered to you the most.

"You aren't everyone." A muscle jerked in his jaw. "You *aren't* dying." His head bent toward her. "You scared me."

She didn't think anything scared him.

His lips brushed against hers. "You were dying in my arms. There was nothing I could do."

Tears stung her eyes. Her father had died in her arms.

"Come back to me."

Those harsh, rumbling words had her blinking.

And getting lost in the gold of his gaze.

"You think I don't know," Drew began as he eased ever closer to her, "when you leave me? I can tell when you slip into your mind, into the past that has left those scars inside you." His lips thinned. "I don't like it. Don't focus on whatever the hell happened to you. Focus on now. On me."

He kissed her again. Harder. This wasn't a kiss of comfort. This was a kiss of pure, wild need.

His mouth didn't hesitate—it took. He was demanding a response from her and, raw and vulnerable from all that had happened, Tina had no barriers to protect herself from him.

So she just…let go.

Her mouth met his. Hungry. Desperate.

Her hands came up and locked around his shoulders. She pulled him against her. She needed him as close as she could get him.

Her heart pounded. Ached.

When he kissed her, she didn't feel weak. She felt sensual, powerful, *alive.*

Nothing else mattered in that instant. Desire twisted through her; a want that couldn't be denied. Her breasts ached, her legs shifted restlessly. She needed to be closer to him.

Needed…*him.* Her short nails dug into his arms.

His mouth pulled from hers. Just a whisper of a space

separated their lips as he growled, "Stay with me." He began to kiss her neck.

Her breath was fast, it was—

He stilled. "Are you okay? What am I doing?"

And, just like that, he'd done the one thing she'd feared. He'd discovered that she was weak.

So now he was treating her as if she'd shatter too easily.

He stepped back, a hurried, almost clumsy move for a man who usually moved with such grace.

"Tina? Tina, answer me. Are you all right?"

She'd been more than all right a few seconds ago. Unfortunately reality was back. "Kissing me doesn't kill me." She'd had other men who treated her as though she was some kind of broken china doll once they'd seen her attack.

His eyes narrowed. "I didn't…" His hands fisted and he backed up another step. "I don't mean to be so rough with you."

She didn't want him to back away. "I don't need you to treat me like I'm…I'm going to shatter."

He stared back at her. Drew seemed to absorb what she said as his eyes narrowed and swept over her face. "I won't make the mistake again."

She jumped off the bed. She could taste him on her lips. Desire still pulsed through her blood. A desire that seemed to burn too hot and fast whenever they touched. Was it from the adrenaline? The danger? Something else? "What is happening between us?" Then Tina forced herself to say the painful truth. "You didn't even notice me before that group took me prisoner—"

He caught her hand. His head moved in a hard, negative shake. "That's bull. I noticed you every moment."

He sure hadn't seemed to see her. Only when he'd been in the lab with her for his checkups, and then he'd been gruff. All business. Never lingering to chat or—

One dark brow rose. "Calling me a liar?" His head tilted to the right as he studied her. "Doc, I've wanted you in my bed from the first moment I saw you. I came into your office, expecting some kind of quick clearance check from a stuffy M.D., and the next thing I knew...you were in every dream I had."

She sure hadn't expected that. He'd treated her with the same icy indifference that he seemed to show everyone at the EOD.

"Yeah, I noticed you," he continued, his voice seeming to deepen with memories. "But I knew that you were afraid of me, so I stood back."

She didn't deny her fear. What would have been the point? He was a dangerous man. A man who could kill as easily as most men could kiss. There were shadows that clung to him—and always would.

"You're still afraid," he charged, "but I'm done with stepping back. You're not going to get away from me now."

She hadn't been the one stepping back a few moments ago. She'd been the one digging her nails into him. Drew had put the brakes on things. Before she could speak, someone was rapping at the door.

Tina's gaze jumped to the door. It swung open and Dylan, looking at little singed and blistered, came striding inside.

"That perfect timing again," Drew muttered. "Work on it, man. Work. On. It."

Tina frowned at him.

Dylan lifted a plastic bag and seemed to focus just on Tina. "I've got new clothes for you. The doctors here said they'd give you medicine to take with us. They wanted you to stay but—"

"It's too dangerous," Tina finished. She understood. The longer she stayed, the easier it would be for her location to be compromised. It was too hard to keep secrets in a place as public as a hospital. "Does that man—Anton Devast—think I'm dead?"

If he thought she'd died in the explosion, then she'd be free. Wouldn't she? His men wouldn't look for her any longer, and she wouldn't have to be worried about waking up in the night to discover a gun pressed to her head.

But Dylan's tense expression shot down those hopes. "He's not going to believe that, not if he had a man on the scene. And a guy like Devast…he doesn't take chances. He would have wanted to *see* you die."

Great. She snatched the bag from him. So much for being safe again. Safety wasn't going to come easily.

"Mercer received a call." This detail came from a watchful Drew. "Right before the explosion, Devast called his private line and told Mercer that you were about to die."

Her cheeks felt a little numb. Even she didn't know Mercer's private line, and she'd worked for the guy ever since she'd finished her residency. "That's how you knew what was happening. Why you ran to me—"

Drew nodded. "Devast's man must have told him that you were on the plane. He knew we were at that airport and that you were getting ready to take off."

"In order to place the bomb," Dylan said with a roll of his shoulders, "they had to know *before* our team got on scene. They tapped into the EOD system, and they figured out your most likely departure spot."

Then they'd placed the bomb and waited for her to board the plane.

She would have been on board when the bomb detonated, if she hadn't stopped to talk to Drew once more. If she hadn't tried to tell him thank-you before she left.

And if he hadn't promised her—

*Naked bodies.*

So much for delivering on that promise. She was still waiting.

Tina cleared her throat. She was feeling a draft in the back of her gown, and she needed to get dressed ASAP. First, though, she demanded, "What happens now? Am I still headed back for D.C.?" This was her life, and she needed to pick up the pieces and keep going.

Dylan slanted a fast glance toward Drew.

She didn't like that secretive glance. "What happens now?" Tina repeated, the words a little sharper.

"Devast got his start by making bombs, dirty devices that he'd place for the highest bidder." Dylan spoke slowly. "He loves to use his fire to destroy anyone or anything in his path."

So she'd figured out with that up-close brush with death. She'd felt the scorch of fire all along her skin as she was propelled through the air.

"He burned down the ranch his group was using out in Texas."

"HAVOC," Drew said.

Dylan's head jerked in a nod.

Tina frowned as she tried to understand. "So he creates havoc, that's his big thing?"

"No." Drew exhaled slowly. "He *is* HAVOC. It's a terrorist group. They're global, and their main goal is destruction. Devast started the group. He used his bombs to create it from fire and destruction and fear. He's a threat that needs to be eliminated."

"You're giving me this intel because he keeps coming after me…" Mercer must have finally given them the all-clear to reveal this information. All it had taken was—what?—a few attempts on her life. One attempt that had nearly been too successful. In return for nearly dying, she got HAVOC clearance. *Thanks, Mercer.* Her boss could be a real jerk.

"That's not why we're telling you." The intensity in Drew's voice worried her.

Her bare feet curved over the cold floor. She waited.

"We're telling you because we need your help," Dylan said. "The EOD needs you."

"What?" Sure, if they needed her to patch up the wounded, then Tina was their girl. But if they were talking about a mission in the field… "No, no, you've got the wrong woman—"

"That was the problem," Dylan continued roughly. "You weren't the woman who was supposed to be picked up as bait. Another EOD agent was. Rachel was the bait who should have been taken, but Devast followed the wrong trail of breadcrumbs."

Drew's lips were a thin, grim line. "You weren't ever supposed to be brought into this mess. Hell, you didn't even have a tracker on you! There was no way we thought that HAVOC would ever come after you."

A tracker. She stiffened. Tina had placed trackers in plenty of agents. The small devices were inserted right under the skin, a precaution in case of capture. The EOD could follow the signal sent from the tracker and locate the agent almost any place.

"Once we realized Drew had left the ranch, we activated his tracker. That's how we got to you both so fast in Lightning. Before Drew and Sarah checked in, we were already en route." Dylan's face tightened. "I'm sorry you were brought into this mess. It wasn't supposed to be you."

"But now it is." She was tangled up in HAVOC without any chance of escape.

Dylan nodded. "And now we need your help."

"Dylan…" A warning edge entered Drew's voice.

Dylan's gaze flashed. "The orders came from Mercer. As long as Devast is out there, she's not going to be safe." He jaw hardened as he stared at Drew. "Do you want that? Do you truly want her to be constantly at risk, always looking over her shoulder, always wondering when another attack might come?"

Drew's hands fisted.

Tina clutched the bag of clothes a bit tighter. "What is it that you want me to do?"

Dylan focused back on Tina. "We don't want you to run. We don't want to hide you."

Drew swore. "I told you already. I *don't* like this plan. We have other options that can work."

"Nothing that we can do now. Nothing that will be as effective as—"

"As what?" Tina demanded.

Dylan hesitated a moment, then said, "We want you to help us catch Devast."

"She's still alive."

Anton didn't let his expression alter when he heard this news. "That is disappointing. You'd…assured me that she was on the plane."

"That agent—he stopped her. I thought she'd already gotten on board, but the guy stopped her for some damn sweet talk." Disgust thickened the words as they drifted over the phone line. "Those two must be involved. I don't know how the hell I missed that."

"Apparently, Agent Lancaster is a man who is very good at keeping secrets." Drew Lancaster…not Stone Creed. That had just been an alias the agent used when he got close to HAVOC. Now Devast understood who the fellow truly was. And it was time to unearth every secret Drew Lancaster possessed.

*Know your enemy.* When you knew your enemy, it was easy to attack his weak spots.

"They took Tina Jamison to a local hospital then they cleared out of the place. But don't worry, I'll find them. Just give me a little time."

Anton sighed. Why did everyone always think that he would tolerate failure? "Time isn't on your side. You'd better find them, fast." But he was already talking to a dead man. Whether this man delivered Tina Jamison or not, he was dead.

Anton had no use for traitors. Men like the agent on the phone...they'd sell out anyone.

He stared down at the photo on the desk in front of him. Drew Lancaster.

He'd already managed to pull up some records on the man. Born in a small Mississippi town, abandoned by his father. The guy had been trouble as a kid, thrown in and out of juvenile halls. He was always running from the law.

Lancaster's mother had worked herself to death.

And Drew Lancaster...he'd fought his way out of that life and joined the army.

Became very, very good at killing.

Anton hung up the phone and kept staring at Drew Lancaster's image. A man who'd come from nothing. Who existed only to kill.

Right now, Drew Lancaster was one of Mercer's attack dogs, but, as Anton had already discovered, some of Mercer's men could be bought...if the price was right.

Anton was good at making the price right.

He smiled as he stared down at Lancaster. Another dead man, one who just didn't know it yet.

But, before Drew Lancaster died, Anton planned to use him.

Use him, then dispose of him.

# Chapter Seven

The Dallas skyline stretched in front of Drew. He stared at the buildings, noting the sweep of architecture as it bled into the red evening sky.

He and Tina were in a plush hotel room. Five star all the way. No dusty sheets or wobbly chairs would be found in this place. For security, Drew had requested two adjoining rooms. Dylan and Rachel were stationed right down the hall in another set of adjoining rooms.

Dylan was determined to go through with Mercer's ridiculous plan. They wanted Tina to continue with the deception of being Mercer's daughter. Wanted her to play that part—and to keep Anton's focus on her—until their team could bring down HAVOC and its leader.

He hated that plan. Tina wasn't trained for a situation such as this one. Putting her into the middle of this fight could very well get her killed.

*I won't have her death on my hands.*

The door squeaked open behind him.

Soft footsteps came toward him.

He kept staring out at the setting sun. Its light reflected off the high-rise towers.

The scent of strawberries drifted in the air.

His fingers curled into fists. "Why did you say yes?"

Because she had, and with that one word, Tina had changed everything.

She'd agreed to Dylan's too-dangerous plan, and she'd made saving her even harder.

"I agreed because Devast is determined to kill me, and no matter what you do or say, he isn't going to believe I'm not Mercer's daughter."

*My fault.* That burned like acid in his gut. He and his team had thought they were being so smart.

Mercer's real daughter, Cassidy Sherridan, had needed to vanish. Intel had leaked out about her—not her specific name, but the fact that Mercer had a daughter he'd hidden for years—and the sharks had started to circle. They'd needed to get the sharks off their blood scent.

*We needed bait.*

But the bait was supposed to be Rachel. Not Tina.

They'd left a trail of evidence including phone calls and a log of private meetings connecting Rachel and Mercer. They'd wanted all those circling sharks to think that Rachel was the one connected so intimately to Mercer.

When the sharks came in to attack, Rachel and the team would have been ready.

But the main shark had gone after the wrong prey in New Orleans. Tina had been down there—why?—and Devast had connected her to Mercer.

"I'm sorry," he told Tina, and he meant the words. Drew was sorry that he'd screwed up her life, and that his team had brought her into this twisted mess. He turned toward her.

She stood just a few feet away, her eyes wide, her cheeks a soft pink.

*She's so beautiful. Does she even realize what she does to me?*

He cleared his throat. "Why were you in New Orleans? You weren't supposed to be there."

"The call came down that an EOD doctor might be needed on scene." Her smile was wry. "Considering some of the locations the agents travel to, visiting New Orleans sounded like a really good option for me. I can't… I can't always go into the field. It was—"

"Safe," he finished as he edged toward her.

She nodded. Her hair brushed across her cheeks with that slight movement. "I thought that would be the perfect trip for me. I needed a break from D.C." A rough laugh eased from her. "I guess I got my break."

"A break is one thing." He tried to keep his anger and fear leashed. "Signing on to *finish* this mission? That's something altogether different. You're risking your life." The anger spiked, sharp and hard, within him. "You don't belong in the field, Doc. You need to get back in an office. Go back to—"

"I know his daughter."

Hell. He'd wondered if Tina had put the puzzle pieces together. The woman was sharp. She'd been working in the EOD office when Cassidy Sherridan had gone in a few months back. Cassidy hadn't headed to the office willingly. She'd been hunted, nearly shot right outside on the street in front of the EOD office.

"She's trying to escape, isn't she?" Tina asked.

Yes, Cassidy wanted out of the prison that had held her in check for her entire life. "Not at the cost of someone else's life." Cassidy would never go for a plan like that.

"It's not just about her." Her gaze seemed shadowed. Since when did Tina keep secrets from him? "I want to stop Devast, too. I want to help."

He had to touch her. He shouldn't. She was still recovering but…

His fingers trailed down her cheek. Like warm silk. "Help by staying alive."

"I can do *more.*" Now she had anger of her own pushing through the words. "So I'm not an agent. I've been working with the EOD for years. I can keep a level head. I won't panic. I have my medicine now, so I can control my attacks. I can *do* this."

The problem was that he didn't want her to "do this." What he wanted was for her to be far away from danger. He forced his hand away from her and took a step back so the scent of strawberries wouldn't be so tempting. "Go to your room. You should get some rest." He turned away.

"*Stop it.*"

That wasn't anger coming from Tina. It was full-on fury.

He glanced over his shoulder.

Her cheeks weren't just a soft pink any longer. They were flushed a dark red. "Uh, Tina…"

"I don't take orders from you, Lancaster. Whether I'm completing this mission or not—that isn't your call. It's mine. It's my life."

"A life that you could lose!"

"Pierce Hodges already lost his life."

Pierce. His body tensed. Pierce Hodges had been the pilot on that plane. A good guy. Drew had worked with him before and—

"Pierce died because Devast was coming after me. Devast is going to keep coming. If we don't stop him, innocent people are going to die."

This was what she didn't seem to get. "You're innocent."

Tina shook his head. "Not in his eyes. You really think you're going to be able to convince him that he made a mistake? My life has been bound with Mercer's since I was eighteen. You were trying to link him to Rachel, but you overlooked the fact that he's been linked with *me* for too long."

*Eighteen?*

"I won't have more deaths on me. Not when I can do something to stop this."

"You don't know what you'll be facing—"

Her chin lifted. "Maybe you don't remember, but when we were in that hellish room and that jerk with the knife was getting ready to cut me—when he was getting ready to take a finger from me—I didn't make a sound."

He shook his head. He didn't want to remember that moment. It twisted his guts.

"I'm not going to crumble. I don't have your training, I get that. But I can do my part."

He stared back at her.

Her eyelashes flickered. "I know what this is about."

He doubted it. He was good at keeping his secrets.

She stalked toward him, stabbed her index finger into his chest. "It's because of the attack I had. You can't get past it."

Drew shook his head. "That's not—"

"I am not some little piece of fluff. Do you understand me? Yes, I had an asthma attack. My asthma gets severe—especially if smoke is billowing around me! But I've got it under control. I'm fine now."

But he'd never forget how terrified he'd been. "I'm not going to risk—"

Her finger stopped its stabbing, but her eyes were bright with fury. "I'm not yours to risk, Agent."

*I feel like you are.*

"I told you already. This is *my* life."

But he felt like she was his.

"You think I'm some green girl who doesn't know

what she's doing? That I'm just a healer. That's what you said, right?"

There wasn't any "just" about it. She saved lives. She'd saved plenty of agents. That was damn important.

"I killed a man when I was eighteen."

There was that magic number again, only now he realized it was attached to a dark story that had changed her life.

"I can do it again, if I have to."

She'd killed a man? His doc? Drew shook his head.

Her smile was sad. "Anyone can kill, under the right circumstances. Those circumstances..." The smile vanished as she swallowed. "They didn't give me a choice."

His heart was pounding in his chest, racing fast, but when Drew spoke, his voice came out flat. "What happened?" He had to know. It was getting to the point where he felt as though he had to know everything about her.

She backed up a step.

He caught her wrist, held her there. "What happened?" She didn't get to drop a bombshell like this one and just walk away from him.

She straightened her spine. Her whole body seemed to tense as if she were bracing herself for the memory. "It's one of those 'wrong place, wrong time' stories. They always end badly, you know."

Pain echoed in her voice and seemed to strike right at his heart.

"My parents and I got caught in the middle of a bank robbery. When we walked into that bank, we didn't realize what was happening until we heard the teller scream."

She eased out a slow breath and continued. "My dad, he was a cop. He had his dress blues on that day. He always looked so good in them. My mom would call him her 'handsome cop.' And he did look handsome that day. I was proud of him. Always so proud."

She pushed her left hand through her hair. Her eyes were on his, but Drew didn't think Tina was actually seeing him. Her gaze seemed to be focused only on the pain of the past. "We went inside, thinking that we'd be in and out. We had dinner reservations at six that night." She pushed out a hard breath. "We didn't make dinner."

"Tina…"

"As soon as they saw my dad, the robbers panicked. They screamed for him to get on the ground and to lift his hands up."

He wanted her in his arms. But Drew didn't move.

His thumb rubbed lightly against her wrist. The beating of her pulse seemed to steady him.

"I had an attack. They were worse back then. I used to get them more frequently." Her breath eased out slowly. "My dad always carried medicine for me. He was reaching for it, but the robbers thought he was reaching for his gun."

Hell.

"They shot him. My mother ran at them and they shot her, too." Tears glimmered in her eyes. "My mother died instantly, but my father didn't. His blood was all over me, and there wasn't anything I could do. I was trying to pull in air, begging them to help my dad, and when I looked up—" She blinked and finally seemed to see Drew once more. "The shooter had his gun pointed right at my head."

Drew didn't speak. He found that, for once, he couldn't.

"Sirens were screaming. Help was coming, but it wasn't going to get there fast enough. I knew I'd die. Just like my mom. I didn't want to die."

Every muscle in his body had locked.

"I had been trying to stop the blood from flowing out of my dad. My hand was just inches from his holster—from the gun that he had never grabbed." A tear slipped from her eye. He carefully wiped it away. "I lifted it and I fired, right before the shooter did. I killed him."

"You saved yourself." Eighteen. He'd never imagined that her life had been so dark. No, he hadn't wanted it to be dark. He'd always liked to think that only good things happened to the doc. *She's my good thing.*

But it seemed danger had stalked her for far longer than he'd realized.

"What happened to your dad?" he forced himself to ask.

"He died right after the police stormed inside."

Hell.

"Mercer was there."

So this was how Mercer fit into the puzzle of her life.

"He and my dad…they were friends. He was at the funeral. He stayed with me, made sure that I was set for college. Med school."

Med school. He understood. "You wanted to be able to save lives."

"I did but…I still couldn't save that man at Lightning. No matter what, you can't save everyone."

She pulled away from him; headed for the connecting door. The room immediately seemed colder without her near.

Tina paused and glanced back at him. "I didn't tell you that story so that you'd feel sorry for me."

"Sorry isn't what I feel." She was even stronger than he'd thought.

*And I always thought she was damn tough.*

"You can't save everyone," she said again as she gazed back at him. "You should have realized that by now."

He had. He wasn't interested in saving everyone.

*Just her.*

"You don't know what's going to happen next. You don't

know if you can save me. Whether I agree to the plan or not, Devast is hunting me."

*You don't know if you can save me.*

She was right. He didn't know. He had no idea how this case would end.

Tina slipped into her room then quietly shut the door.

He stood there, far too aware of the silence around him.

After a few moments Drew found himself staring down at his own hands. Tina had killed one man. He didn't want to remember all of the lives he'd taken.

*She's my one good thing.*

His head lifted. He looked toward that connecting door. Then Drew took a breath and a step. He kept walking until he was in front of that door.

He didn't knock. Didn't hesitate. He just swung that door right open.

If it hadn't been unlocked, he probably would have broken the damn thing down.

Tina stood near the bed. When the door bounced against the wall, she spun toward Drew and her eyes flared wide with surprise.

"I know that I have to try to save you." He felt as if a force was pulling him toward her. A moth to the burning flame. She was the fire he craved. "Because I need you." Then he kissed her.

With the press of his mouth to hers, Drew got that fire.

The desire seemed to ignite in his blood. Her mouth was soft and warm, and she kissed him back eagerly.

This wasn't a time for fear. Not a time for death.

This was their time.

"I made you a promise," he growled against her mouth. "There's something you should know. I always keep my promises."

"So do I," she whispered back. Her hands were between

them, seeming to singe him right through the thin fabric of his T-shirt. Then she was shoving up that T-shirt.

He tossed the thing across the room. "No going back," Drew told her, voice rough. He was rough.

She was silk.

"I don't want to go back."

With those words, Tina sealed both their fates.

He lifted her and put her in the middle of that big bed with its clean, white sheets. Her hair spread out behind her.

She reached up for him.

She was the most perfect thing he'd ever seen. And this time, for her, because it was *her,* he was going to show her that he could be more than the wild lover who consumed.

Though he sure as hell wanted to consume her.

He stripped the hotel robe off her. Let it drop to the floor. Her breasts were round and perfect, with light pink nipples. He put his mouth on her and tasted. "Strawberries..." he whispered. His arousal shoved hard against his jeans.

She arched her hips toward him. "That's my...ah... lotion. I found some in the gift...ah—shop!"

He made a mental note to buy her a case of strawberry lotion. "Love that scent on you." He loved touching her, kissing her. His lips feathered over her flesh. He licked her nipple, caressed her and held tight to the reins of his control.

He was trying to be gentle and easy.

Tina wasn't.

Her nails raked over his back. Her fingers pushed between them and fumbled with the zipper of his jeans.

"I don't want to wait," she told him. "All I want is *you.*"

Her voice was the best sin he'd ever heard. She was every thought he had right then.

He ditched his jeans, but made sure to keep the protection he'd shoved into his back pocket. Yeah, he'd visited that gift shop, too. *Because I knew I wouldn't be able to keep my hands off her.*

And protecting her, always, was his priority.

His hands pushed her thighs farther apart. Drew nearly lost his mind when he touched her and found her so ready for him. He took care of the small foil packet in a flash.

He heaved in a deep breath—*hold on to your control, hold on to it!*—and positioned himself at the entrance to her body.

He started to thrust into her, but then Drew stilled and she glanced at him. Tina's eyes were wide and eager, her lips parted. Desire was on her face. Desire wasn't enough.

He wanted to see her pleasure.

"No going back," he said again. This moment would change everything for them. She needed to realize that. This wasn't just some adrenaline-infused hook-up sex.

Tina's hands caught his. Their fingers threaded together.

He thrust.

*Too good.* Drew growled out her name. He withdrew, thrust again. Her legs wrapped around his hips. The pleasure built, rushing fast and hard toward him. This wasn't just sex. He'd had sex with plenty of other women.

This was more. So much more.

He thrust faster. Harder. His control ripped. No, shredded.

He'd wanted to show her that he could be a considerate lover.

But he was starving for her.

Her sex squeezed around him. He was staring straight into her eyes, and he saw her gaze go bright and blind with pleasure.

His climax hit him. The pleasure slammed through him, took his breath, and he held on to her as tightly as he could.

Drew kept thrusting. The pleasure wasn't ending. His back tightened. His muscles strained. Tina whispered his name. She was so beautiful. So perfect to him.

The release crested. The surge was the most powerful climax he'd ever had.

When it ended, when the shudders stopped racking their bodies, Drew could only think—

*No going back.*

He always kept his promises.


I T WAS THE ringing of the phone that woke Drew hours later. The steady peal came from his phone, a weak and low sound since he had fallen asleep in Tina's room.

In her bed.

He glanced over at her. His arm was curled around her stomach. Her lashes swept over her cheeks. She breathed easily. Slowly.

The phone kept ringing.

Drew slipped from the bed. He yanked on his jeans and padded quietly to his room. He grabbed for the phone.

He didn't recognize the number, but in the EOD, that didn't mean anything. Burner phones and untraceable cells were used every day. "Hello?"

"Agent...*Lancaster?*"

He turned away from Tina's door and headed toward the skyline view. Darkness had fallen over the city now, but the lights from the skyscrapers still gleamed. "Who is this?"

"I believe you've been looking for me," the voice said. It was a male's voice. No accent. No inflection. "And I've been looking for you."

He glanced toward the connecting door. He could still see Tina in there. Safe in bed. "I think you've got the wrong number." His gut clenched and his body went on high alert.

Laughter. The cold kind. "No, I've got the right number, and I've got the right man."

Drew strained to hear any background noise that might give the guy's location away, but, unfortunately, he heard nothing.

"How valuable is she?" the voice asked him, still as calm and easy-as-you-please.

"Sorry, man, I don't know what you're talking about." His voice came out the same way. He could play this game all night long.

Devast. The big boss had actually called him. Called him on what should have been a secure line. Who was giving the guy this intel? They'd thought that the EOD had outed its traitor months back. A guy in the tech department who was now in a cold grave.

Someone else was on Devast's side. The bombing on that plane and Devast's access to his personal number proved it.

A sigh drifted to his ear. "Don't waste my time, Agent Lancaster. I know exactly who you are. You know who I am. And you know what I want."

*Tina.*

Fine. His cover was blown with the guy, so he could cut through the bull. "You're not getting her."

The laughter came again. "Why? Because it's your *job* to keep her safe?" A taunt.

"Something like that." He made sure to step away from the glass and yank the curtains closed. He was up so high that Devast shouldn't be able to take a shot at him, but Drew had never been the type to take chances.

"I've learned a lot about you recently. After you killed my men, I had no choice but to learn."

The guy spoke of death far too easily. But then, Devast

had been an instrument of death for most of his life. "You sure don't seem upset about losing them."

"And you don't seem upset about killing them."

Once more, his gaze returned to Tina's still form in that bed. She thought that she was safe right then.

She wasn't.

Drew couldn't track the call—he didn't have the equipment handy—but was Devast tracking *him?* Right then? The HAVOC network was massive. And inside the EOD. "This call is over," he said. He wasn't going to risk revealing Tina's location to—

"I want to make you an offer," Devast said quickly. "Consider it a business deal. You give me what I want, and I'll give you a million dollars."

What? One million dollars was one hell of an offer.

"Like I said," Devast continued, and now the guy sounded way too confident. "I learned a lot about you. I know that you're a man who would once do anything for money. Lie. Cheat. Steal. And now…for Mercer…for *his* money, you kill."

His back teeth had locked. "You don't know as much about me as you seem to think." He didn't auction off his services to the highest bidder.

"Give me what I want," Devast said, "and I'll give you enough money to finally kick all of that poor Mississippi mud off your shoes."

The bedcovers rustled softly from the other room. He turned away from the room and hunched his shoulders. "Who says there is anything wrong with that mud?"

Silence. Then… "Think about my offer. Think long hard about it. I'm giving you one chance. The money—and your life."

For Tina's life.

"I don't give second chances, Agent Lancaster. This is your one opportunity. Be smart. Take it."

The floor squeaked behind him. The scent of strawberries drifted in the air.

"Bring her to me. Forty-eight nineteen Demopolis Way. The old factory on the east end."

Devast sure thought he'd found Drew's price. "When?"

"Sunset. That will give you plenty of time to get her away from the other agents."

And it would give Devast plenty of time to lay his trap. Drew was no fool.

*I won't betray her.*

The floor gave another low squeak. Tina would be close enough to hear every word that Drew said. "I'm surprised you don't just want me to kill her right now."

He heard the sharp, indrawn breath behind him.

"I won't have another mistake on my hands. I want to *see* Mercer's daughter die."

Drew turned his head. He could look straight into Tina's eyes then.

"Make the trade, Agent Lancaster."

The line went dead in his ear.

Fear flashed in her eyes. "Drew, what's happening?"

He glanced down at his phone. Had Devast traced them? And if the EOD traitor had hacked into the system already... There could be no safe place for her.

No safe place, but with him. Drew rushed toward her and locked his fingers with hers. "We need to leave *now.*"

ANTON DEVAST SMILED as he put down the phone. The seed had been planted. Now, it was just about letting it take root.

Drew Lancaster could trade the woman. Or he could die.

A simple enough offer.

Anton looked to the right. Dallas waited. So did his prize.

*When I'm done, I'll send you a piece of her, Mercer.*

Then his old friend would know that they'd finally come full circle.

A child for a child.

Payback.


MERCER STARED DOWN at the faded headstone. Weeds were trying to grow over it, so he bent and jerked them back.

The stone was cold to the touch.

No flowers. No mementos marked the grave.

The man buried there had been gone for nearly twenty years. No one but Mercer ever came to visit the grave. He knew—he'd had eyes on this cemetery for years.

"Who is he?"

He didn't glance back at the agent's curious voice. He was bringing Cooper Marshall on to the case because he needed backup. The mission was going to get tough, Anton wouldn't hesitate to kill—and Cooper Marshall, well, he was an agent who never hesitated.

He was also a guy who didn't seem to understand fear. Sometimes that lack of fear was a weakness.

Sometimes it was an advantage.

"He was a man who got caught in the cross fire." A cross fire that had come from Mercer. "And his death started a war that I need to end."

He backed away from the grave. His gaze slid around the area. The spot hadn't changed much in twenty years. The trees were still heavy, lush. A pretty spot.

Jon might have liked it.

Grief pulled at him, but Mercer pushed the memories away. "You've been briefed on the situation with Dr. Jamison?"

He couldn't bring in a full force of agents on this case. The more people who knew, the more potential for word to spread about his "daughter"—and that couldn't happen.

He'd already sent a message to Cale Lane, his real daughter's husband. The agent was on high alert, and he had strict orders to keep Cassidy out of the U.S. until this nightmare was over. Cale also had orders *not* to tell Cassidy what was happening. If she thought that someone else was being risked in her place...

*Cassidy would be back here in an instant.*

He didn't want her in that kind of danger. He'd begun the whole ruse with Rachel Mancini to protect Cassidy.

The plan had been for Rachel to draw out his enemies—in particular, Devast. The agents would have taken Devast down, and Mercer's "daughter" would have died in the cross fire. They'd arranged to stage Rachel's death so perfectly.

With that fake death, the hunt for his daughter would have ended. Cassidy would have been safe to live a normal life. A life she'd never had before.

But now that perfect plan was in ashes.

"I have been briefed, sir," Cooper replied.

Mercer's gaze slid to him. "Dr. Jamison has volunteered to assist in the rest of the investigation. She wants to help us catch the man behind her abduction."

"Anton Devast," Cooper said. His blue stare drifted to the grave—and to the name on the headstone.

*Jonathan Devast.*

"Devast is a very dangerous, unpredictable man." Mercer cocked his head as he studied Cooper. "You're rather unpredictable, too." A point that had almost kept the man out of the EOD.

Cooper Marshall was an ex-U.S. Air Force Pararescueman. He jumped into danger any chance he could get. Literally.

A faint smile lifted Cooper's lips. "Yes, sir, I've been told that I am."

They were alone in the graveyard. No eyes. No ears. "You've been on a mission in Afghanistan for the past seven months." Mercer exhaled a slow breath. "And I have someone who has been in my agency, someone who has been selling secrets, straight to Devast. Since I personally sent the plane to pick you up on your mission—"

"You think I'm not the traitor."

"I *know* you're not." He knew every single secret that Cooper Marshall possessed. He should. The man was family.

Some secrets, Cooper didn't even know.

"So you want me to go in and join the others who are already on point," Cooper began.

Mercer shook his head. "No, I don't want you making any contact with the other agents."

Cooper's blond brows rose. The sunlight glinted off his hair. *Not as golden as my Cassidy's. Much darker.*

Cooper cleared his throat. "Sorry. I'm a little confused. If I'm not to join the team, then just what is my assignment?"

"To make sure you're not seen. To follow Tina Jamison. To keep your eyes on her and to report to me anything or anyone that threatens her."

"And the agents with her— What, you don't trust them? You think one of them could be the traitor?"

He wanted to trust them. On paper, Drew Lancaster, Rachel Mancini and Dylan Foxx were all good agents.

But somewhere in the EOD, there was an agent who was selling him out.

So, yes, he wanted to trust them, but he'd learned long

ago that he didn't always get what he wanted. And he wouldn't put Tina's life in jeopardy. "Money can tempt a man to do just about anything in this world." The right offer, to the right man… "This isn't the first time that one of the EOD's own has turned." Not the first time and, unfortunately, not the last. When you moved in the circles that he did, betrayal was a fact of life.

It was a fact that had killed his wife.

It had taken time, but Mercer had traced that brutal attack back to the man who'd been his friend.

His gaze returned to the grave.

"I want extra protection on Tina Jamison. She's not an agent, and I'm not going to have her sacrifice her life because she's trying—" He stopped because Cooper had no reason to know the rest. *Tina is trying to repay a debt to me.*

He knew exactly what Tina was doing. Because he knew her. Tina was smart, incredibly so. She always had been. Her father had kept smiling pictures of a young Tina— holding her slew of academic awards—all over his desk.

Mercer had never been able to show pictures of his own daughter. But he had one of Cassidy, one that he carefully hid from others.

Cassidy and her mother, Marguerite.

Tina was grateful to him. He knew that. She'd told him time and again. But he hadn't done anything for her. She would have graduated college on her own. Gone to med school—*on her own.*

Sometimes, he felt as though all he'd done was put her in a cage. He'd offered her the position at the EOD because she was a damn good doctor.

But… *Did I also offer her the job so that I could keep an eye on her? To protect her, the way her father would have done?*

Only, Mercer's protection had turned into a trap.

*The same way I trapped Cassidy.*

And if he'd known about Cooper Marshall sooner…

He shoved out a hard breath. "You're on Dr. Jamison's security detail. You watch her. You protect her. If you think she's compromised, you move immediately to retrieve her." He leveled his stare at Cooper to make sure the man got the point. "Your priority isn't bringing down Devast. It's keeping Dr. Jamison alive." Because if a choice had to be made…

Cooper nodded.

Then Mercer wanted his agent to make the right choice.

## Chapter Eight

"He wants a trade," Drew said as he paced the small confines of the house.

A safe house, or so he'd said. The guy had hustled her out of that big hotel fast. Told her that their location had been compromised.

Then he and the other two agents had burned some serious rubber getting to this new spot.

A spot that was a lot less glamorous than their five-star hotel. The little neighborhood had looked abandoned at first glance. Houses in disrepair, roofs slumping, windows boarded up.

The streets were dark, and Tina sure hadn't seen anyone walking in the area.

Tina glanced around the small, single-story house. There were burglar bars on the windows. Instead of making her feel safe, they just made her feel like a prisoner.

"Tina, did you hear me?" Drew paced toward her. A frown pulled his dark brows low. "The SOB called me. I don't even know how the hell he got my number—"

"Sydney's working on that," Rachel murmured. There was a dark bruise on her temple. A cut on her cheek. Little mementos from the explosion that had nearly killed her and Tina. "She thinks someone hacked into the system because he called Mercer's private line, too. She'll find the link back to the hacker, just give her some time."

"We don't have time." Dylan looked as grim as Drew. "What we have is a terrorist who's locked on us. He's killed to get to Tina already, and he'll do it again. He won't hesitate to take out anyone in his way."

Was that why they were on that forgotten street? To minimize any collateral damage? The hotel had been full, right in the middle of the bustling city, but the houses on the street were pitch-black and empty.

"We have to be prepared for his attack," Dylan said. "It could come at any moment."

Tina found her gaze sliding back to Drew. He'd been quiet, too reserved, since they'd left the hotel. "What aren't you telling me?" There was something else, she knew it.

"A killer is after you!" It was Rachel who answered a little too quickly. "Isn't that enough, Tina?"

No, right then, it wasn't. "What kind of trade did he offer?"

"One million dollars." Drew's gaze was guarded. "For you."

One million— "Didn't realize I was worth so much." She had to ask because morbid curiosity compelled her. "Is that alive...or dead?"

His pupils widened, the dark spreading into the gold as he stared at her. "Alive." The word seemed to drip ice. "I guess, after what happened before, he wants to kill you personally. To make sure the job gets done."

The man who stood in front of her— *I feel like I don't know him.* With his careful words, his dark gaze and his expressionless face...this wasn't the man who'd made love to her so passionately. As if he couldn't get enough of her.

This was the tough agent. The one with ice in his veins. She hadn't...expected to see this agent return. Not after what had happened between them. She hadn't wanted to see him again.

Tina squared her shoulders. So much for not going back. He seemed to have flipped their relationship right back to the starting point on her. All thanks to one phone call. "Then I guess this is our chance."

"Are you sure?" Dylan asked. "Before we go too far, we can—"

"We've already gone too far." Every time she shut her eyes, she saw the plane exploding around her. *I'm so sorry, Pierce.* She kept thinking about the pilot. Was his family waiting for him to come home? Had they already learned of his death?

Her eyes stung, but Tina blinked quickly, refusing to let any tears fall. She could be strong now. She *had* to be. Tina lifted her hand and adjusted her glasses. Rachel had brought them to her. She'd even given Tina a backup pair in case these got smashed.

The backup glasses were in her bag. Right next to Tina's inhaler. *I won't be going anywhere without it.*

When the HAVOC group had taken her from the hotel, they sure hadn't stopped long enough for her to get her medicine. But she would *not* be that vulnerable with them again.

*Can't be vulnerable. Won't.* "I need a gun."

The breath expelled from Drew in a hard rush. "You need to think about this. We can get to Devast another way."

"What way?" She rose from the chair and paced around the room. The familiar weight of her glasses strangely reassured her. "How long has the EOD been trying to get Devast?"

"Years," was the mutter from Dylan. "We got lucky when Drew was able to infiltrate the group. Their main pilot was caught in an explosion a few months back—one of their own bombs—and they were desperate for another pilot."

And in stepped Drew.

"You're not going to get so 'lucky' again," Tina said. "Devast will be even more suspicious of new faces now." She wasn't saying anything they didn't already know. "If we want to take him down, I'm the ticket that you can use. I'm the one who will get up-close access to the man." She forced a smile even as she wiped her damp palms on her jeans. "So how does this work? He calls Drew again—"

"He already told me when and where to make the exchange."

She blinked. "Well, then, you just have to tell Mercer. His men will be there, and the trap will be sprung." A relieved smile spread over her lips. This agent business wasn't as hard as she'd thought. "He's caught himself."

Drew shook his head. Then he walked slowly toward her. He stopped less than a foot away. She could feel the warmth of his body surrounding her. "It's not that simple, Doc."

When he said "Doc," the word dripped and rolled. It sent a shiver over her.

He called her doc the way some men might call their girlfriends sweetheart or baby.

Emotion was breaking through his mask once more, and she sure was glad to see the real Drew. "Then tell me how it's harder."

"If he picks the location, if we go by what he says, then we could walk right into a place that Devast has already got wired. He'll blow it up and kill every agent there."

"All while he stays back, nice and protected," Rachel added. She'd taken a seat on the old couch.

Dylan stood close to her. He always seemed to be close

to Rachel. "We don't go by Devast's rules. We make him come to us."

"So…what? You're saying that if we go by his orders, the guy probably wouldn't even be at the exchange?" She'd just have a bomb waiting for her?

Drew shook his head. "I'm saying we aren't ready for the meeting yet. I have to guarantee that Devast will be there. To do that, I have to *make* the trade personal."

She glanced toward the burglar bars. "Did he know we were in the hotel?" Was that why they'd rushed out so desperately?

"He had my phone number. Devast called me and deliberately kept me on the line long enough for a trace." Drew shrugged. "It was a safe bet. Only a fool would have stayed put then. I wasn't just going to wait for the hotel to explode beneath my feet."

She swallowed. No, Drew wasn't a fool. And she wasn't exactly game for anything exploding beneath her feet.

*Make this personal.* "What are Devast's weaknesses?" Tina asked as she tried to figure out a plan. "He has to have them, right? Everyone has a weakness."

"If he has one," Rachel sighed, "then we haven't found it."

Drew's phone rang.

Tina glanced down at it. He'd placed it on the table when they'd entered the safe house.

"Sydney's monitoring his calls. If that's Devast, she'll get a lock on him," Rachel said, eagerness pushing in her voice.

Drew picked up the phone. His face didn't so much as change expressions.

"Syd will get her trace," Tina said, "but Devast will get one on us, too." That was how it worked. But…was that what the agents wanted? "Is this some game of see who hits the fastest?"

"I told you, I have to make this more personal for him." Drew pushed the button to activate the speaker on his phone. "Calling me again already?" She was surprised by the mocking tone of his voice.

Laughter filled the room. Chill bumps rose on Tina's arms.

"You left the hotel so fast, Agent Lancaster. Did you truly think that you could run from me?"

Drew's gaze focused on Tina.

"I'm a step ahead of you," that hard voice said. "Your bars won't keep her safe. And if you won't give her to me, then I'll just take her."

*Your bars.*

He knew where they were.

Rachel had leaped to her feet. Her gun was out and she was at the window on the right, carefully searching the area outside.

"Doctors, police officers, even agents…they can all be bought."

Drew hadn't taken his eyes off Tina. "You haven't named the right price for me," Drew said. "You haven't bought me."

Silence.

"Why pay, when I can get her for free now? Thank you for showing me exactly where she was."

"Come on and try to take her." There was no fear in Drew's voice at all. Just a dark challenge. "Let's see how fast your men die. I took 'em out before, and I'll do it again."

"We'll see…"

"Yeah, we will. You want her—then you're going to have to *track* me yourself." A deliberate taunt.

Then the call was over, just like that. Dylan had gone to the back of the house, and Drew closed in on Tina.

"Does he know? He said 'bars' as if he could see where we were." She fisted her shaking fingers. "And when am I going to get a weapon? *When?*" If Devast was about to come storming into their not-so-safe house, she needed a weapon.

His hand closed around her shoulders. "You stay by my side, okay? No one is taking you. I've got this worked out."

Oh, great, wonderful to know but before he'd even finished speaking, she heard the eruption of gunfire. The fast blasts came from the back of the house.

Tina flinched.

"Two men!" Dylan called out.

"Three up front!" Rachel said at the same moment.

Devast hadn't been lying. He had found them. Trailed them? But they'd been so careful when they'd left the hotel. They'd switched vehicles, left false trails… "How did he do it? How did he track us?" Even if he'd had a trace on the phone call, he shouldn't have been there so quickly. It took time to triangulate signals and then to actually get an attack force to the right location.

*But his team was already here. He didn't have to wait for a lock on the phone.*

Devast shouldn't have been able to find them.

Unless…

Tina's eyes widened. The GPS trackers. The trackers implanted in the agents. If he'd accessed the EOD system, then Devast could have found Drew—and through him, Tina—by following those tracking signals.

Rachel was returning fire to their attackers. So was Dylan. Instead of joining the firefight, Drew was trying to pull Tina down the narrow hallway. She dug in her heels, then she ducked when a bullet whipped by her. She fell to the floor and her hands slapped against the hard wood.

Tina looked up. Drew had dropped with her. She met his stare even as a cold knot twisted in her belly. "You said that Devast had hacked into Syd's system?" Just months before, the EOD computer system had come under attack. Agent intel had been compromised.

They'd thought the leak had been controlled but...

*Maybe Syd wasn't looking in all the right areas.*

"If Devast knows you're with me, he could be tracking you," she said. Literally, damn it. He could have a direct feed into the small tracking device that she'd implanted in Drew's back. "If the EOD is compromised," she said as more bullets flew, "then you're compromised." Because Devast had definitely outed his identity. "We have to deactivate the tracker."

The only way to deactivate it was to cut the tracker out of Drew.

"Not yet. I want him tracking me." He grabbed her hand and pulled her down the hallway. "First order of business—*staying alive.*"

*Wait!* He *knew* Devast was following his GPS signal? His mocking challenge for Devast to "track" him made chilling sense to her.

Drew led Tina into a back room. The windows were boarded up. As far as exit strategies went, this sure wasn't looking like a good one to her.

He tossed aside the faded rug that had been spread over the floor.

With the rug gone, Tina easily saw the trapdoor in the floor. "Is that a basement?"

He hauled up the trapdoor. The hinges groaned. "It's our escape plan. You didn't think we'd actually bring you to this place without being sure we could get you out alive?"

The sound of gunfire still thundered from the other rooms. "But what about Rachel and Dylan?"

"They're coming. They're just leaving a little something for Devast." His eyes glittered at her. "We needed to buy some time, so we had to lay the trap."

What?

"After what he said on the phone back at the hotel, I figured he was tracking me, and I wanted that SOB to follow me here." His fingers tightened around the door. "Because here, the guy will realize that he can't just stand back and let his flunkies chase after us."

Rachel and Dylan burst into the room. "They're set. Let's go."

What was set?

"We're going to use some of HAVOC's own techniques against them." Drew took her hand. "There's a tunnel under this house. Stick with me. Stay low."

A tunnel? With dust and mold and— *Breathe. In. Out.* She had her medicine. This was fine. She could handle a tunnel. She had to. Tina nodded quickly and hurried down with him.

There wasn't any dust. No mold, either. Just a small, narrow tunnel, maybe three feet tall and three feet wide. She had to crawl, and she did it, double-timing her movements so that she could get out of there as fast as possible.

The sound of their breathing seemed loud in that small space. Rachel was leading the group. Tina was right behind her, with Drew following close. Dylan closed in the back.

"We're clear," Rachel said. She'd stopped. She shoved open another trapdoor, one that led them into the darkened interior of yet another house.

Tina scrambled from the tunnel. Drew grabbed her hand. "Easy. We're about a quarter of a mile away, and we don't want to do anything that would give away our position."

So they stayed in the dark. She quickly realized that they'd already stocked this house. Food. Water. First-aid equipment. Binoculars. Night-vision equipped, of course. These agents were definitely prepared.

Rachel took the binoculars and peered through the thin blinds that lined a narrow window. "They're surrounding the house. Do it."

"Do what?" Tina asked, almost afraid to find out. Her eyes had adjusted to the darkness enough for Tina to see Dylan pull a small box from his pocket.

"Time for Devast to experience some HAVOC of his own," Drew said. His arm brushed against hers.

Dylan pressed a button. An explosion seemed to rock the street. Through the blinds, Tina saw the flare of fire flash high up into the night.

The house they'd been in had just exploded.

"They're falling back," Rachel whispered.

Yeah, because the fire was driving them back.

Drew's fingers slid down her arm. "He tried to kill you with a bomb before, so we just gave him what he wanted."

She turned toward him, frowning. "Are you sure Devast is going to believe this? You think he'll buy that I'm dead?"

He pulled a knife from the sheath strapped to his ankle. "No, I think the explosion will just make him even angrier. And when he sees my GPS signal moving fast soon, he's going to track it. He'll come after me with everything he's got."

Instead of letting Tina be the bait in this deadly game, Drew was using himself. "Why?" she whispered.

"Because I don't want you in his sights."

And she realized why he hadn't told her about this plan sooner. Because he didn't intend to use her to finish this investigation. She'd agreed to cooperate, but he was the one calling the shots. He wanted her out of Devast's path, and he'd just blown up a house to make sure Devast couldn't get to her.

Drew offered her the knife, handle-first. "I need you to cut the tracker out of me. You know it emits a signal that covers a one-mile radius, not an exact location, so, for the moment he'll think I *could* be in that blaze."

Her fingers closed around the knife. "What are you going to do with the tracker?"

A muscle jerked in his jaw. "Rachel and Dylan are going to take it. They'll lure Devast into Mercer's web, and I'll take you out of here. No signal will link back to you and me. You'll be safe." His eyes glittered at her. "My job is to protect you. That's what I'm doing." He stripped off his shirt and turned his back to her.

Rachel and Dylan hurried into the other room, saying they had to check in with Mercer.

The knife's handle was cold. Her fingers were slippery with sweat. She rose onto her toes. She knew exactly where Drew's tracker was located because she'd been the one to implant it. The blade sliced over his skin.

The guy didn't flinch.

Carefully, she pulled out the tiny device.

"Here." Rachel was back with bandages. Tina gave her the tracker and began to patch up Drew.

"We'll rendezvous just like we planned?" Rachel asked him as she pocketed the tracker.

"Dawn," Drew agreed with a curt nod.

Rachel glanced toward Tina. "This is the best way. Mercer agreed. The big boss wants to make sure Devast can't ever threaten you or anyone else in the EOD ever again." Rachel nodded once more and then she was gone.

Tina smoothed the bandage over Drew's back. The knife was still in her left hand. His blood was on the blade.

Drew turned toward her. "We don't have a lot of time

here. We need to clear out, just in case those guys out there wise up and start searching the houses." He took the knife. Stepped away and dug in a chest of drawers. A moment later he was clad in a fresh shirt and tossing her—a leather jacket?

"I know you like motorcycles," he said with a wry grin.

Uh, no, not so much.

"Time to ride."

Her head was spinning.

"All of the other houses on this street are abandoned. That fire is going to blaze until the EOD tips off the fire department. And Devast's men? They're not leaving until he gives them an order to clear out." He took her hand. "So we leave *them*. The motorcycle is stashed a few blocks away. Ten minutes, and we'll be clear."

She slid on the leather jacket.

Then he gave her a very blond wig.

"Just in case you're spotted." He pulled a baseball cap low over his brow. He'd retrieved the cap from the same drawer that held the jacket. "We can't be the ones they are looking for. That would wreck the plan."

She balled her hair up, secured it, and became a blonde in moments. She also ditched her glasses. Or rather, Drew took them and carefully stored them in his pocket.

A few minutes later they slipped out the back door. She could hear voices yelling, could hear the faint crackle of flames in the distance.

"Stay close to the buildings. Stay close to me," Drew whispered into her ear.

Right. She had this.

Her fingers shoved into the pocket of the leather jacket and they curled around—medicine?

She felt the familiar shape. An inhaler. Drew had made sure that she had an inhaler close by.

Their footsteps were silent as they snaked through alleys and around old houses. The area looked so abandoned but she knew they couldn't take any chances.

Drew caught her in his arms. He spun her around and pressed her back into a brick wall.

"What's happening—" Tina began.

Drew put his lips on hers. He kissed her hard and deep, and his body seemed to completely surround hers.

Then she heard the thud of footsteps advancing toward them.

Drew's hand moved between their bodies. His fingers brushed over her stomach. What was he doing? There? This didn't seem like the place to—

His lips pulled from hers. He kissed her jaw, brought his mouth to her ear.

"I've got my gun," he said.

Oh. *That* was what he'd been reaching for.

The footsteps were coming closer. They hadn't gotten away clean, after all. So much for the grand plan.

"Get a room!" an angry voice called out.

Then the thudding of those footsteps continued as they rushed past Tina and Drew.

Tina glanced up. She saw the back of a man's head. He had a baseball cap on, too. He was rounding the corner, not seeming to care about her and Drew at all.

Her shoulders slumped in relief.

"We're almost there." Drew's body still brushed against hers. "You ready?"

Tina swallowed and nodded. She glanced once more toward the left, but the other guy in the baseball cap was long gone.

Her fingers curled around Drew's. They hurried into the darkness.

It seemed to take forever, but in reality, Tina knew only

about five minutes had passed before they were on the promised motorcycle. The bike vibrated between her legs when Drew kicked the engine to life. The motorcycle shot into the night. She held on tight to Drew.

And they got the hell out of there.


COOPER MARSHALL WATCHED the lights of the motorcycle vanish as he pulled his baseball cap lower over his forehead.

He had his own ride waiting, but he didn't want to follow Drew Lancaster too closely.

He hadn't realized that Drew and Tina would be coming down that alley. He'd seen the flames and thought that he'd been too late to help the doctor.

*Nice job getting her out of there.* He had to hand it to Lancaster—the agent had a certain style.

And Cooper knew that he'd been lucky, too—if there had been more light in that alley, Drew would have recognized him.

Recognition wasn't on Mercer's agenda. Not then.

He wondered if Mercer knew just how involved Drew had gotten with the good doctor. Because Cooper had seen the way the guy touched her.

The touch of a lover, not an agent.

He'd have to brief Mercer. Drew might not be up to his usual standards of ice and detachment on this particular case.

When cases got personal, they all too often got messy.

As far as Cooper was concerned, personal involvement always led to danger.

Tina Jamison was already in enough danger as it was.


"I DIDN'T GIVE any order for a bomb!" Anton snarled. "What the hell happened?" He wanted to shatter the phone.

"B-boss, the house just exploded. They were inside—all of 'em! They've got to be dead."

His back teeth ground together. He spun around and tapped on his keyboard. The feed on Drew Lancaster's tracker immediately came up. According to the signal, Drew Lancaster was moving fast down Bridge Avenue.

His eyes narrowed. *I've got you.* Drew thought that he could throw up a distraction and escape with Anton's prey?

Not happening.

The agent should have taken the money. Now he'd just die.

*And so will the woman.*

TINA'S ARMS WERE locked around Drew's waist.

He eased the motorcycle to a stop, pulling it up near the wall of a bar. It was hitting close to 3:00 a.m., and the bar was about to shut down.

Perfect timing for him.

Drew shoved down the motorcycle's kickstand.

"Why are we stopping here?" Tina asked quietly.

He knew the place didn't look like much of a safe house, but that was why they were there. Appearances could be plenty deceiving.

He tucked his helmet under his arm. "You need a place to crash." They both did. "By morning, this case will be all over." Because Devast would have followed their bread-crumbs straight to Mercer.

Drew had told Tina that he had to make the situation *personal* for Devast. And he had. The bomb at the house on Moyers would have infuriated Devast. As soon as Devast had pulled up Drew's tracking signal and realized that he'd escaped the flames…

The SOB would have decided that he had to go after Drew himself.

After all, Devast had told him that he didn't give second chances. Devast's men weren't catching Drew and Tina.

*So you have to get involved in the job yourself, don't you, Devast?*

Devast would follow their planted trail. Mercer and the EOD agents could capture him.

And Tina would be able to head back to her old life.

He pushed open the bar's door. His gaze swept the area, checking for any threats and, when he was satisfied, Drew gave a nod to the bartender. The redhead raised her brows when she saw him. Like Sarah, this woman had ties to the EOD. The bartender's brown gaze flickered toward the Staff door.

A band was playing. A somebody-did-me-wrong slow tune. Three couples were still on the dusty dance floor.

Drew eased past them. Tina glanced over at the couples, hesitating.

"Come on, Doc," he said. "We need to go."

A sad little smile tilted her lips, but she followed him. Just past the Staff door, a narrow flight of stairs waited for them. Drew had actually been to this bar a time or two before. He'd crashed here between missions, so he knew exactly how to find the hidden key to the upstairs apartment. They headed inside, and he secured the door.

"The bar will close by four," he told her, putting the motorcycle helmets down. "Then it will be dead quiet, and you can have plenty of time to rest."

That same smile—one that looked a little sad and a little lost—curved her lips as Tina ditched her blond wig. "And when I wake up again, I'll go back to my old life?"

He nodded. "That's the plan." A fast and frantic plan that he'd had to make as soon as he realized exactly how Devast must be tracking them.

The music drifted lightly in the room, muted, so that he

couldn't clearly hear the singer's words, but he could easily hear the guitar's strains. The low melody was sad and soft.

Tina brushed her hand through her hair. "I never thought so much could change for me in just a few days."

"You'll be back to safety soon."

"Safety." She seemed to be tasting the word. "Yes, I guess I will be safe again." She glanced toward the bed. Narrow, only built for one.

Drew cleared his throat. "You take the bed." He could crash in the chair. *If* he could crash. Ever since he'd gotten that call from Devast, his body had been tight with tension and too much adrenaline.

*He's not the first person who thinks he can buy my allegiance.*

But this wasn't about allegiance. Not really.

It was about Tina.

There were some things in this world that money would never be able to buy.

Tina didn't advance toward the bed. Instead she turned and walked closer to Drew.

The tension in his body got even worse. Hell, if the woman was about to try her hand at seducing him, she wasn't going to need to try too hard.

Any time she got close to him, desire pushed through him and he *wanted*. Not an easy need. Frantic and fast. Consuming. Not safe, when safety was what she seemed to need so badly.

"Drew…"

The way she said his name had him clenching his hands into fists. Husky, sexy. She'd been running for her life that night. He needed to back off, but if she was saying—

"Will you dance with me?"

That was not what he'd expected the doc to say. Drew just stared at her.

Then he saw the color flood her cheeks. The embarrassment because she thought he was rejecting her.

"Never mind." She spun away from him. "That was stupid. I—"

He caught her shoulders in his hands and slowly pulled her around to face him. "I'm not much of a dancer."

Her lashes lifted. She gazed up into his eyes. "Neither am I."

No, she didn't understand. "My life is about missions and violence. Following orders and getting the job done." His left hand slid down to the curve of her waist. His right caught her hand and cradled her fingers in his.

Her breasts brushed against his chest as she stepped closer to him. Her scent filled his head. Strawberries shouldn't make a man feel drunk, but her scent worked better than wine on him.

"There wasn't a lot of dancing when I was young," he confessed to her. The music was still playing from downstairs. "There wasn't a whole lot of anything." Except a kid on the path of destruction. A mother with a heart that was breaking because she couldn't seem to stop her son.

His feet moved. Slowly. Carefully. "I won't ever be the polished guy." Not the one who could blend in at any party or ball.

Her movements matched his. But she wasn't awkward. She was graceful and perfect.

His doc.

He took his time, trying to give her what she wanted because making her happy mattered to him.

"There's more to you," Tina said softly as she glanced up at him with eyes that seemed to gaze right into his soul, "than just bullets and combat."

She didn't understand. It was the combat that had saved him. "When I was eighteen..." His fingers tightened around hers. At eighteen, Tina had watched her parents die. And at eighteen, Drew had been trying to find his life. "I had a choice. Get my life in order, join the army, or find myself in jail."

"Jail?"

"I told you before I wasn't the good guy back then." He'd been the guy always looking for trouble, and finding it. "I was on a crash course with destruction. I knew what waited in my future, and it wasn't pretty."

"Why?" No judgment. No censure. Just curiosity. "What was happening to you?"

The music kept playing. So he kept dancing with her, bringing her even closer to his body as they moved so slowly around that little room.

"My old man didn't want to be a father, and my town… Hell, 'poor' didn't even describe it. There was no way out for us. My mom was trying, but she couldn't make enough to take care of me and my three sisters."

For an instant she stilled.

"Crime was the way to make money for them. So I did whatever I could. Whatever I had to do. The only law I followed was my own."

He waited for her to stop looking at him with such trust in her eyes.

Only, she didn't.

They kept dancing.

"I stole," he confessed. "I cheated. I found myself in the back of a patrol car a dozen times."

"What made you change?"

The money had been good. He'd finally been able to buy nice clothes for his sisters. For his mother. *My mom…* "My mother cried over me. When the cops came—when they were taking me back to juvie—she begged me to stop."

He could still see her tears. "I wanted to help her, but all I was doing was hurting her worse."

"I'm sorry," Tina whispered.

Drew shook his head. He wasn't telling her the tale because he wanted her pity. Pity was the last thing he wanted from her. "I wanted her to be proud, not to be holding her head down in shame because of what I was doing."

Then Drew realized why he was telling Tina about his past, when he'd tried to bury those Mississippi memories as deeply as he could.

He wanted Tina to know that he couldn't be bought, not anymore. That he wasn't going to trade her for money.

That he was better than that.

He pulled in a deep breath. "I joined the army. I sent her my checks. She used them for the girls." Kim, Heather and Paige. "Things started to change for my family. Things changed for *me*."

Did she understand?

"I'm not the same boy I was back then."

Tina shook her head. "I never thought you were."

And it was still there. That blind trust in her eyes. When she'd been on that godforsaken rooftop and Lee had put his gun to her head, Tina had looked over and seen Drew. She'd recognized him, even when he'd had on that damn ski mask.

Trust had been in her stare then, too.

"Why do you have so much faith in me?" She shouldn't. It was dangerous. *He* was dangerous. "You know about my missions." She'd dug the bullets out of him, seen the scars from the knife attacks. "You know everything I've done."

"Yes, I do." She pushed up onto her tiptoes then. Her mouth brushed against his.

She knew, and Tina wasn't afraid. She wanted him—good, bad and everything in between.

And he just *wanted her*.

His mouth pressed harder on hers. Need and desire twisted within him. He licked her lower lip, and loved the little moan that she gave in response.

They weren't dancing any longer. They were at the edge of that too-small bed.

Tina's hand slid down his chest, rested over his heart.

"Before I get my safe life back," she whispered against his lips, "I want to be with you again."

Nothing could have stopped him from being with her.

The bed groaned beneath them, the old mattress and springs buckled. He didn't care. He stripped her, kissed her, caressed every silken inch of her body.

She put her mouth on his neck. Sucked. Licked. Made him shudder and ache.

He'd used all of his control before.

This time, in this moment, knowing that she was going to slip away from him soon…

There was no control.

There were frantic hands. Deep kisses. Clothes that were tossed to the floor.

He stroked her everywhere. Couldn't stop touching her. He had to see all of her.

He tasted Tina. Every single inch of her. Her fingers sank into his hair and she arched against him.

When the first release hit her, he tasted her pleasure.

When the second hit, he was *in* her, driving as fast and as hard as he could. He'd pulled away from her only long enough to grab protection from his wallet, and even leaving her for that long had made sweat break out on his forehead.

Again and again he thrust into her.

The bed slammed into the wall. Her hips arched toward him.

His fingers were locked with hers. Their bodies moved in perfect rhythm.

Tina stiffened beneath him. Then her legs curled around his hips and she held him even tighter as pleasure flew across her face.

The release crested, thundered over him, and left Drew growling her name.

His heart thudded, racing too fast in his chest, and his breaths shuddered out.

Tina smiled up at him.

Such damn trust.

He was afraid he'd destroy it. The way he'd destroyed too many other things in his life.

*I don't want to destroy her.*

Because she was coming to be the one thing in his life that mattered the most.

THE TRACKING SIGNAL had stopped. Devast had followed Drew Lancaster's tracker all the way to the outskirts of the city. An old factory, one that sat, abandoned, boarded-up, with the faint light of dawn just touching its weathered roof.

No cars were outside. No vehicles of any sort.

Devast stared up at the factory. So this was to be the endgame location. Interesting choice.

Mercer must truly think that he was a fool.

*You shouldn't underestimate me, Mercer.* That mistake would be fatal.

Anton would show his old friend.

He parked his car. He'd come alone. There was no sense losing any more men on this mission. Not when he knew exactly what he was doing.

*Delivering a message.*

Some messages were best delivered in person.

Anton headed toward the main entrance. This moment had been such a long time coming. Anton made sure that his steps were slow. Made sure to lean heavily on his cane. After all, he was frail. He was weak.

Very helpfully, someone had undone the chain that sealed that main entrance.

He heaved the chain out of his way. Deliberately, he wrestled with the chain as if it were a struggle to lift its weight. The chain fell to the ground. He pushed against the door. Once. Twice.

Then the door was sliding open. Anton waved the dust aside and entered the factory.

Silence.

Darkness.

"I know you're here!" Anton called out. His voice seemed to echo back to him. "Why must we play these games?"

Footsteps padded behind him. In front of him. To the left— The right—

And they attacked.

A gun was shoved into his back. A knife put to his throat.

"Got you," a man's hard voice snarled.

Anton shrugged. "So it would appear." But he wasn't interested in talking with a flunky. He wanted to see one man. *Needed* to see him. "Where's Mercer?"

Because he knew that Mercer would have been pulled out of his office. For a case this personal, there would be no sitting on the sidelines for him.

Lights flickered on in the factory. One after another, flashing on in rows.

Anton didn't even blink at the onset of all that too-bright illumination in a factory that should have been without power for years.

*I know how appearances can deceive.* Hadn't he been the one to first teach Mercer that lesson?

Anton's gaze cut to the left. The man with the knife had short, dark hair and a gaze that said he'd seen plenty of death.

Good. Then there would be no surprises when he saw it again.

Anton pounded his cane against the floor. "I asked for Mercer." He let his shoulders hunch inward. A frail old man was what he appeared to be. "I know…he's here…" He huffed out a ragged breath. "Where…is…he?"

"Right here, Anton." Mercer's strong voice rang out.

Then he was there. The devil himself was striding from behind the old machinery and walking so confidently toward Anton.

*You think you've won.*

It was time for the man to see exactly what he'd lost.

Anton hunched forward even more. The knife was cutting into his throat, but he didn't care. He'd never minded a bit of blood.

He wasn't the squeamish sort.

But then, neither was Bruce Mercer.

He clutched his cane then jerked it up in a flash. Before the knife could slash his jugular, he drove the handle of his cane into the man's side. The man stumbled back, but Anton was already attacking a second time.

He whirled around. Pushed the handle of his cane to deploy his own blade—

And he drove that blade into the stomach of the fool who'd pulled a gun on him.

The gun discharged. The bullet drove into Anton's chest.

Good thing he'd been wearing a bulletproof vest.

He laughed when the second agent fell. He was still laughing when he turned to face Mercer—

And the gun that Mercer had aimed right between Anton's eyes.

"Rachel?"

Ah, yes, that would be the agent with the knife—now he seemed to be desperately trying to save his partner.

Pity. Anton had sliced her nice and deep. Saving her might prove difficult.

"It's over, Anton," Mercer said, voice flat and hard. "You're done."

Hardly. "Actually, I'm just getting started." But he dropped his cane and raised his arms as if surrendering. "Can't just kill me now, can you?" Mercer and his code of honor. He wouldn't shoot an unarmed man in the head.

Mercer's gaze glittered. "Yes, I can."

Anton lost his smile. "That would be a pity. Because then you'd be killing *three* innocent women."

Mercer hesitated.

Right. The code of honor. It would be the death of Mercer. Just not at that moment.

Others had to die first. What good was revenge if your victim didn't suffer?

"Where is Agent Lancaster?" Anton glanced around the factory. He expected more agents to swarm him.

They didn't. Others were there, but they were hanging back. No doubt, by Mercer's order.

"Shouldn't he be here for this little party?" Anton asked. Lancaster had lured him there. The agent must have stashed Mercer's daughter first, then headed to this factory.

Clever, but not clever enough. Anton would get to her, soon.

Mercer reached into his pocket and tossed something at Anton's feet.

"We need an ambulance!" The other agent. Still so

frantic. He must really care for the woman—hadn't he called her Rachel?—dying in his arms.

Mercer tapped the transmitter on his ear and barked a command for help.

Ah, maybe Lancaster would come in with that aid.

Anton's gaze slid back to the object Mercer had tossed toward him. He squinted, then realized—

"Agent Lancaster isn't here. He never was," Mercer told him.

Anton laughed. "Well played." *Not well enough.*

Footsteps rushed inside toward him. More agents came in the door and a few EMTs appeared with them.

He slanted a glance toward the injured agent. A pretty woman, but one currently bleeding out on the dirty floor. "Better get her to a hospital," he advised, rather helpfully, he thought. "Or that will just be another death, on *you,* Mercer."

Mercer's fingers tightened on the gun. "You're done, Anton. No more bombs. No more threats. No more deaths."

Someone snapped handcuffs on his wrists. The metal bit into his skin.

Anton shook his head. "It's a pity that Lancaster wasn't here, but how about you deliver a message to him?"

Mercer marched toward him. When they were good and close, Mercer lowered his voice and said, "It was an accident. You know it was. Why the hell did you start on this path?"

*Not an accident. A life lost. Payback.* "Tell Lancaster that I know his price now."

"Agent Lancaster doesn't have a price." Disgust thickened Mercer's tone. "Get him out of here," he ordered as he stepped back and motioned to his men. "Maximum security. We're going to—"

"Three lives," Anton said as hard hands grabbed on to

him. "The first woman will die in three hours. The second in six, and the third in nine. One life, every three hours."

Mercer jerked his hand in the air and the motion froze the agents who were trying to drag Anton toward the door. "What the hell are you talking about?" Mercer demanded.

Pleasure filled Anton. Oh, but he'd finally found a way to break his old friend. And he'd use the man's own agent to do it. "Agent Lancaster's price. I told him that I wanted your daughter. Instead of delivering her, he hid her from me."

"I don't have a daughter," Mercer snapped.

"Of course, you do. Marguerite's daughter. Beautiful Marguerite." He could see her so clearly in his mind. "She died for you."

"You *killed* her." A muscle flexed in Mercer's jaw. His eyes blazed. Ah, but the mask was falling away. The real man—the real monster—glared at Anton.

"You're missing the point," Anton said as the memories flared in his mind. Painful, dark memories. "And you're costing Lancaster time that he doesn't have. One woman, every three hours…"

"What women? Who are they?"

This was the fun part. The part that would set his plan into real motion. "Lancaster's sisters. I have them. And my men will kill them, unless I get exactly what I want."

# Chapter Nine

"The music has stopped," Tina said softly. She wasn't even sure when it had stopped. She'd been too caught up in Drew.

In the pleasure that he gave to her.

They were in bed. Tangled together. His heart beat beneath her hand, and the steady rhythm made her feel safe.

But that was the way Drew always made her feel.

*He says I'm going back to my safe life. But I am safe, right here. Right now. With him.*

She pressed a kiss to his shoulder. Then a kiss to the scar that cut across his cheek. He'd gotten that scar on his first mission with the EOD. The first but not even close to the only battle wound he'd received.

He'd suffered. He'd survived.

His fingers brushed over her jaw. "Tell me this... Why the hell does a girl like you want someone like me?"

She frowned at that. *Someone like me.* "Because you're a good man." Strong. Brave. Sexy.

"You should be running as far and fast from me as you can," he said, shaking his head. His hair looked so dark against the white pillow. "Not letting me touch you. Because, Doc, every time I touch you, I want more."

Her throat seemed to go dry at that. "Good, because you make me want more, too." Maybe—maybe they could have more. There had to be some way for them to work things out. Dawn had come. She could see the faint light trickling through the windows. Devast would be in custody by now. She'd be clear. Drew's current mission would be over.

Maybe they could take some time together. She'd like that. Being with him… *Yes.* She'd definitely be game for more time with Drew.

A hard knock shook the door.

Tension slipped into Tina's body. Their last few surprise visits hadn't exactly gone well.

"It's okay," Drew said as he eased from the bed. "I didn't bring a phone because I wanted to make sure I wasn't traced. That's Kelly from downstairs. She was going to tell us when we were clear."

Right. Clear. The nightmare was over.

Drew pulled on his clothes. Tina didn't want to be found naked in that room, so she fumbled to quickly dress, too.

The pounding came again. Harder. More desperate.

"Open up!" a woman's voice shouted. "I've got orders— They need you, Drew.*"*

The Drew that had been in Tina's arms moments before seemed to vanish. At the woman's tense words, all emotion left his face as he hurried toward the door.

Tina yanked her shirt into place and hauled up her jeans.

Drew pulled open the door.

Tina caught sight of the pretty redhead who stood on the threshold. "There's a problem," the woman said. "A big problem."

"Devast got away." Drew yanked a hand through his hair. "I knew that SOB was tricky. He's not getting his hands on Tina, though. I'm not going to let him—"

"They have Devast." The redhead's brown stare darted to Tina then slid back to Drew. "But Devast… He says that he has your sisters."

Drew shook his head. He took a step back.

Tina reached for him. "Drew—"

He flinched away from her. "That's not possible. The bastard is just bluffing. Playing another of his games."

The redhead paled a bit more. "Mercer doesn't think so. He wants you to come and meet him. The women…" Now her gaze held sympathy. "He says they are going to start dying soon, unless Devast gets what he wants."

Tina glanced down. Drew's fingers were clenched so tightly that the knuckles were white. "What does he want?" Tina whispered.

She glanced up at the silence that followed her question. The redhead was staring right at her.

"You," the woman said. "If Drew trades you, then Anton said that his sisters will be let go."

THE ELEVATOR DINGED, the doors opened and Drew stormed through the third floor of the Dallas FBI office. Tina was at his side, as if he would have left her with anyone else. His mind was a mess of chaos and fury, but one thought remained constant—*must protect her.*

Rage was building inside him, cracking through his surface. His sisters? He hadn't seen them in more than a year. He tried not to bring his darkness to their doors because he knew that he had enemies.

He sent them money. Had been sending those checks to his family ever since his enlistment. Every month, just like clockwork. His mother had passed away a few years ago, but he hadn't stopped his checks. He just wanted to help his family.

*But now they might be in danger...because of me.*

His fingers squeezed Tina's even tighter. She seemed to be his only link to sanity right then.

*Maybe he's lying.* That had been Tina's response to

Kelly's dark announcement. *You don't know yet, Drew.*
*Let's find out what's going on.*

He'd find out all right.

Kelly had told them to meet Mercer at the FBI office.
Mercer had pulled his strings—as usual—and taken over
the third floor of the building.

Agents rose at his approach, their gazes suspicious.
Yeah, he knew he probably looked like hell right then,
and he wasn't in the mood for any bull.

One FBI agent made the mistake of stepping into his
path.

Drew tensed, ready to swing.

"Easy." Mercer's voice boomed out. "Agent Lancaster
isn't someone you want to tangle with."

The FBI suit backed up.

Drew marched toward his boss. "Where's Devast?"

Mercer pointed down the hallway. "We've got him in
secure holding. Two agents in the room with him. Two at
the door. He's not going any place."

"Does he have Drew's sisters?" Tina asked, her voice
soft and worried.

Mercer focused on her. "I'm sorry you were brought into
this mess, Dr. Jamison." He pulled her away from Drew.
"Rest assured that you are safe now. Devast will not be
threatening you again."

But Tina shook her head. "Don't 'Dr. Jamison' me,"
she replied crisply, notching her chin up into the air. "We
usually play that game, but not now. I'm not going to
pretend—" She sucked in a deep breath and squared her
shoulders. *"Does he have Drew's sisters?"*

Mercer's stare slid back to Drew. After a tense beat he
quietly said, "We've confirmed that your sisters are missing."

Drew fell back a step. *Kim. Heather. Paige.*

"We haven't confirmed that Devast has them yet. He came to the factory, with no backup, no men in sight, and he said—"

"I want to talk to him." Because Drew would find out in five seconds if Devast was telling the truth or if he was just spinning another web of lies.

Mercer nodded. He pointed down the hall. "The second room. There's a two-way mirror in there so that—"

"Watch what happens, I don't care." Drew had to force the words past a tight throat. The darkness of his life should never have touched his sisters. Never.

Kim was planning a wedding.

Heather... Heather had just started a new teaching job.

And the baby of the family... Paige had entered college two months ago. He'd sent her some extra money, just in case she needed—

"Don't kill him." Mercer's hard voice had Drew's head snapping up. "Do you hear me, Agent? Do. Not. Kill. Devast. That's an order."

*Mercer thinks Devast is telling the truth.*

"Drew..." Tina stepped in front of him. "What can I do?"

"Nothing." *The rage was cracking the ice.* "If he has them, I'll find out where they are." He'd get them back.

He walked around Tina. She didn't follow him. The two agents at the holding room door tensed when they saw him approach.

"Let him in," Mercer ordered from behind Drew.

They stepped to the side.

Drew shoved open the door. Anton Devast was seated at a small table. Both of his wrists were cuffed to the table's legs. He lifted his head at Drew's approach and smiled.

"Ready to make a deal with me now, Agent Lancaster?" Anton asked quietly. "I know your price."

TINA STARED THROUGH the observation glass. Her whole body was so stiff with tension that she ached. Mercer was by her side, quiet, intense, his gaze on the scene unfolding.

"You don't know anything about me," Drew said to Devast. His voice was cold and empty, totally lacking feeling.

*This is the agent they whispered about. The one with ice in his veins.*

Anton Devast, old, frail, but with evil seeming to ooze from his pores, shook his head. "I know plenty. You're a man who thinks that he needs to atone for the past. You try to wash the blood from your hands but you just can't."

As Tina watched, Drew placed his hands on the table and leaned toward Anton. "The EOD caught you. You aren't going to blow up any more buildings. You're not going to destroy any more lives. You walked into our trap. Followed every breadcrumb that we left for you, and now you're trying to throw out some desperate, last-minute—"

"Mercer can't locate your sisters, can he?" Anton's voice was mild, but the smile on his face was satisfied. "I'm sure he said that it's just a temporary situation. That he has agents on the ground in Mississippi, and that he *will* find them." Anton shook his head. "I gave him a timeline. I told him, one woman, every three hours. There's not a lot of time left before the first woman dies."

Tina turned stunned eyes on Mercer. "Why didn't you tell—?"

"We can't negotiate with terrorists," Mercer said flatly, but she saw the emotion in his eyes. The storm of anger. "Anton Devast is a terrorist wanted in over a dozen countries. We won't agree to any of his demands." He shook his head. "Especially when that demand involves killing an EOD employee."

*Me.*

"I want proof of life."

Her attention jerked back toward the glass when Drew said those five cold words.

Anton's smile widened. "I thought you would say that. Proof is coming. Mercer will be getting a call any moment."

Drew kept staring at the killer. "If you have them, if you hurt my sisters in any way, I will see you dead in the ground."

One dark brow lifted as Anton stared back at him. "It was your mistake. Any pain they feel is on you. I offered you fair money. You should have taken it and walked away." Anton gave a little shrug, as much of a shrug as his handcuffs would allow. "You could have even sent the money to the women, the way you send all the other checks to them."

"Hell," Mercer snapped, "that's it." He ran a shaking hand over his face. "That's how he found them. He followed the money trail Lancaster left behind."

Tina wanted to rush into that room with Drew. She wanted to *help* him. She'd thought the nightmare was over, but now Drew was facing the hardest fight of his life. "His sisters are all he has." He'd tried to control the emotion when he talked about them, but his voice had broken when he referred to the "girls." Without them, Drew would be lost.

Drew straightened to his full, imposing height as he glared down at the cuffed man. "I'm going to destroy you," he said.

"Promises, promises," Anton taunted. He wasn't even sweating. Surrounded by guards. Captured by the EOD. But still smug.

"He's calling the shots," Tina whispered. Because he held all the power.

"I can't negotiate," Mercer said again.

Her gaze slid to him. Cool under fire, Mercer was

sweating. As she watched him, Mercer hurriedly pulled out his phone.

"Sydney is already monitoring my phone from D.C. Any call that comes in, she'll be able to trace it back to the source. If that bastard really does try to send proof of life, we'll find them."

The door opened. Drew stood there, shoulders tense. "Have you gotten a call?"

Mercer shook his head. "He's playing with us. He knows that we have him, and he's just trying for one last mind game."

Tina wanted to believe that—

Mercer's phone rang.

Drew surged forward.

Mercer stared down at his phone. Tina was close enough to see the Unknown Number message flash across the screen. Mercer put the phone to his ear.

Tina could clearly hear the scream that broke across the line.

Drew yanked the phone away from the EOD boss. He hit the speaker button and the scream seemed to echo in the room. "Who the hell is this?"

"Drew!" The scream changed into his name. "Drew, please, say that's you! I-it's Paige. They told me that you're going to come and get me. Please come for me! *Please!*"

Drew's gaze didn't stray from the phone. His voice was ice-cold when he said, "When you were seven years old, what did I give you for Christmas?"

"You carved me a jewelry box. It had a…a P on it. We didn't have any money, but you said you'd buy me jewelry for it one day—" She broke off, screaming again.

*"Don't hurt her!"* Drew roared. The ice and control were gone. Only fury and fear remained in his voice.

The line went dead.

Mercer grabbed the phone from him. "Sydney was tracing. She'll get them—"

"Not if the call wasn't long enough." He turned away and stared through the glass at Anton. Anton stared back, as if he could see right through the mirror.

Tina reached for Drew's arm but he jerked away from her touch.

Her hand fisted. "We'll get them back. Whatever we have to do—"

"The EOD doesn't negotiate with terrorists," Drew said. The words were growled. And they were almost word for word exactly what Mercer had said. Drew spoke those words as if repeating some long-memorized rule. Then, whispering, he said again, "The EOD doesn't negotiate with terrorists." His breath sawed out as he glanced toward Mercer. "Consider me out of the damn EOD."

Drew stormed from the room.

"Sydney?" Mercer had the phone to his ear. "Tell me you got them. They gave us proof of life, and we only have an hour left before the first woman dies."

Tina's heart was racing. She pulled in as many deep breaths as she could. Drew was back in the interrogation room.

Anton had his smug smile in place once more. "Talked to your sister, did you?"

"*Where* in Louisiana?" Mercer demanded. "I need specifics, and I need them now."

One man knew specifics. One man knew everything.

The man smiling as he taunted Drew.

Tina rushed for the door. She wasn't going to let this happen. Not to Drew. Not to his sisters.

The agents guarding the room tensed when they saw her. But they knew she'd just been in the observation room with Mercer, and she had treated these EOD agents before.

They understood she wasn't the enemy, so she just said, "Mercer wants me in there as backup."

They weren't used to her lying, so they let her in.

She hurried into the interrogation room just as Anton said, "If you want them alive, then you'll give me what I want."

Tina squared her shoulders. "Here I am."

Drew whirled toward her. *"Tina."*

She didn't look at his face. Right then, she couldn't. Tina focused completely on Anton. "You wanted me, and I'm here."

His smiled faded as his gaze raked her face. "What I want is you dead."

Drew stepped in front of Tina, blocking her from Anton's sight. "You aren't getting what you want."

"Then you don't get to see your sisters alive again." His voice had gone low and rough and mean. "Because if you did want them back alive, you'd be bending down, taking that knife from the sheath you keep strapped to your ankle, and you'd shove it into her heart, right now."

Tina locked her knees.

"I kill her," Drew rasped the words. "Then how do I know you won't still let my sisters die? I'm not a fool. I know how you operate. You turn on everyone that you can. Your only loyalty is to yourself."

The door was shoved open again and it banged against the wall. Tina glanced over her shoulder. Mercer was there, chest heaving. His eyes blazed at her. *"Out!"*

Anton laughed. "Brave is she? Coming in here, getting away from you. Maybe she's more like Marguerite than I first thought."

Marguerite. Tina had heard that name before. Not from Mercer, but from her real father. He'd been talking to Tina's mother once and he'd said, "Bruce won't ever be the same. Losing Marguerite broke him."

Mercer grabbed Tina's wrist. "Come on. I told you—"

*We don't negotiate with terrorists.* "I have a deal," Tina said flatly. "A deal that I want to make."

The room got real quiet. The tension was so thick she could feel it pushing at her.

Tina tugged free of Mercer. She stepped around Drew. And she faced the nightmare in that chair. How many lives had he destroyed?

*You won't destroy any more.*

"You can't be trusted," Tina said simply as she stared at Anton.

"Neither can he," Anton immediately replied as his head jerked toward Mercer. "You think he's so good? That he's on the side of the law?" His lips thinned. "You're losing your life, dear girl, because of him. Because of what he took from me. Your father says that he works for justice— but how was killing my Jonathan justice?"

Mercer shoved past Drew and slammed his fists into the table, sending spider-web-like cracks across the top. "That attack was meant for you! How the hell was I supposed to know you'd brought your boy into that life? *You* were behind the attack on Marguerite. You killed her—"

"She wasn't meant to die!" Anton tried to surge to his feet, but the handcuffs jerked him right back down. "I was taking her. Taking your daughter. It was leverage because you were too close to finding out—"

"That you were a traitorous bastard who'd sold out not one but two countries? Yes, Anton, I figured that out!"

They were fighting over lives long lost. What about the lives still hanging in the balance? "Neither of you can be trusted," Tina said. Her breath rushed in and out. In and out. *"And we're running out of time."*

Anton and Mercer both swung their attention back to her. She focused just on the man who was pulling the puppet strings, even while in EOD custody. "We already know the women are in Louisiana."

His eyes narrowed.

"We'll run the rest of the trace down soon enough." She tried to keep all emotion from her face and eyes, just as the others had done. Maybe she was learning how to be an agent. "Tell us where they are."

Anton glanced toward Drew. "Still haven't gone for the knife yet… I guess you don't care that much for your sisters after all."

"You planned better than this." Tina shook her head as she tried to puzzle through the nightmare. "You wouldn't just count on Drew killing me."

"Drew?" Anton murmured. "How intimate. I thought for sure he'd just be Agent Lancaster."

She'd slipped up.

"Drew and Tina," Anton continued, as if tasting their names. "Perhaps I see now why the sisters don't matter as much. They can't matter as much as a lover."

"Get out," Drew snapped. His eyes pinned Tina and then Mercer. "Both of you." His steps were slow and certain as he advanced around the table and got close to Anton. "Turn off any video feeds. Secure the room. Leave him to me. I won't *negotiate*." He spat out the word. "I'll make him tell me."

"Anton has been tortured before," Mercer said, voice grim.

"You should know," Anton told him with a sly glance Mercer's way. "I won't break."

This had to stop. "Take me. Take Drew. Take us both to the place where you have his sisters. As soon as Drew gets them...y-you can kill me." *Or, a much, much better option—we'll find another way out of this mess by then.*

Mercer grabbed Tina's wrist once more. "You're done here."

No, she wasn't. She kept talking and focusing on Anton. "You have men close by, you have to. A guy like you wouldn't leave anything to chance." She ignored the burn in her chest and spoke even faster as she said, "You knew Agent Lancaster wouldn't just kill me without making sure his sisters were safe. You wanted an exchange— so here's one. Get your men to come in. Take us to the women. Then, I'll—"

"Die?" Anton finished.

"No," Mercer snarled.

"I'll trade my life for theirs," Tina said.

Anton smiled. "I was wondering when someone would finally see reason."

She didn't think this man had seen reason in a very, very long time.

Anton's lips pursed as he seemed to think about her offer. The silence and the tension stretched in the little room until—

"Mercer stays with me," Anton finally said as he inclined his head. "Every minute. I want to see his face when he learns of your death."

He was going to take her offer.

"You and your agent there... I'll tell you exactly where to go. My men don't need to take you there. They'll just be *waiting* for you to arrive."

No, more like waiting for them to walk into a trap, but Tina stayed quiet. He was talking, and that was what she'd wanted him to do.

"They're hidden in a Mardi Gras float graveyard in New Orleans." He rattled off the address easily, almost as if it didn't matter. "You'll find it near the river. Get down there, and only *you two* go in. The place is wired, and if more agents show, my men have orders to detonate. They'll kill the women in an instant."

Tina forced herself to speak through numb lips. "We can't get down there fast enough. The time you gave us—"

He laughed. "Bring me a phone. Mercer's phone will do nicely. I'll tell the men to keep them alive, until you get there."

*We can't believe anything he says.*

"Remember, dear, only you and your agent Lancaster are to go in. Try to send in any cops or other agents first and you'll watch the world explode."

DREW DRAGGED TINA out of the interrogation room. His hold was too hard, too rough, but he couldn't let her go.

He pushed her into the first empty office that he found. His glare made sure no one followed them inside. He slammed the door. Rounded on her. "What the hell are you doing?"

Her cheeks were flushed. Her eyes glittered up at him. "Saving your family."

"By sacrificing yourself?" He wanted to shake her. He wanted to *kill* Anton Devast.

"I'm not going to die." She said the words with total confidence. "We just bought time, and we'll be able to figure this out."

Oh, damn it, that trust again. She had to stop seeing him through rose-colored glasses. *See me for what I am.* "We go in that building, we find them—and we are going to face off against at least a dozen of Anton's men. They aren't just going to let me grab my sisters and walk away. They're going to try to take *you*."

"That's why we will have backup. Anton said that other

agents couldn't go in first. They can be there, though, waiting for the perfect moment to attack—"

She didn't understand. Tina hadn't lived her life, day in and day out, with evil. She wasn't getting the way that men like Anton Devast operated. "The minute we walk in that door, he could order the explosion. End us all in one instant. Backup won't do any good then. There will only be pieces left of us."

Tina flinched.

*I'm hurting her.* He immediately dropped his hold. Stepped back.

"It's not much of a plan," Tina said, voice soft. "But it's the only one I had. Now we know where your sisters are. We have their location. We can get them out."

*And all I have to do is trade your life for theirs.*

"You're not even his daughter." He'd go back in there. Tell Devast the truth—

"That doesn't matter anymore." Then she laughed, and it was a bitter sound, so unlike anything he'd ever heard from Tina. "Actually, maybe the lie is the only thing that *does* matter at this point. Because if Anton thought I wasn't Mercer's real daughter, then your sisters *would* be dead. He wants us in New Orleans. He wants us in that building, and as long as we are still alive—we have a chance."

He hated this. "I don't want you at risk."

She walked toward him and closed the space he'd created. Tina touched his cheek. Her fingers were light against that rough scar. She'd never minded his scars.

*I can't let her die.*

But he couldn't stand aside and let his sisters suffer.

"We won't go in unarmed. We'll get hooked up to EOD surveillance. Mercer and his men can watch our every step. Sharpshooters can be placed around the building." She was speaking so quickly now, her words tumbled together.

"They can learn the locations of Anton's men from us. They can give us backup. We *can* do this."

He pulled her against his body. Put his mouth on hers. Kissed her—hard and deep and desperately.

She was trying to be so confident, but she was wrong. He'd been on so many missions that had gone to hell without warning. You couldn't predict every moment. Could never plan for every contingency.

They were taking the bait Anton offered, but were both of them coming out alive?

It was a long shot.

"I trust you," Tina whispered against his mouth. "We can do this."

She shouldn't trust him. Drew put his forehead against hers. "I don't want to lose you."

"You won't."

No, he wouldn't let her die.

*But I still might lose her.*

The door opened behind her. Mercer stood there, filling the doorway. "This is a suicide mission." His voice was grim. The lines on his face were deeper than Drew had ever seen them.

Tina turned in Drew's arms so that she could face the director. "It's only suicide if we don't come back." Her shoulders brushed against Drew's chest. "We will."

Mercer swallowed. His Adam's apple bobbed. "I never wanted this for you. If your father were here, he'd—"

"My father was a brave man. He wouldn't leave three innocent women to die."

Mercer advanced into the room. "You're innocent."

"They're Drew's sisters." Her voice broke.

Drew's own heart squeezed. She was risking everything—*for him.*

"You're a lot like your father," Mercer whispered. "He

was always so damned proud of you." Mercer straightened his shoulders. His gaze turned to Drew. "I know you'd prefer for your own team to have your back on this one, Lancaster, but Mancini is recovering in the hospital right now. She's out, but Dylan is on his way to the airport. Two other EOD agents—Gunner Ortez and Logan Quinn—will meet you in New Orleans. Gunner is the best damn sharpshooter I have. I want his eyes on that building at all times. On *you*."

Gunner Ortez was Sydney's husband. Drew knew first-hand just how deadly a duo Gunner and Logan Quinn could be. He'd admired their work before—and seen them in ruthless action.

"More personnel will be on the ground," Mercer added. "I'll wire you both. At the first sign that this plan is compromised, you use the code word to call in the troops. Understand? Don't hesitate to call us in."

Drew nodded, but as far as he was concerned the plan had already gone to hell.

"What's the code word?" Tina whispered. Her body trembled against Drew's.

"Escape."

MERCER STARED THROUGH the observation glass. Devast thought he had them dancing on his string.

He was wrong.

Mercer glanced over at Cooper Marshall. "You have your orders."

Only Drew and Tina going into that warehouse? *Hell, no.*

He wasn't about to lose them.

Mercer stared at Anton as he spoke. "Disable the bombs. Take out the suspects. You'll have your own team in place. Use any means necessary." He pulled in a deep breath. "Get the civilians out and make sure that Dr. Jamison comes back alive."

"Yes, sir."

Anton continued to sit there, cuffed but smug.

*He wants to look into my eyes when my daughter dies.*

The same way that the bastard had been looking into Mercer's eyes when he'd found out that Marguerite was dead. Anton had pretended sympathy then.

There was no pretense any longer.

Mercer checked his weapon. The end was coming— for Anton.

## Chapter Ten

They'd gone back to New Orleans. It was strange to return to the city, especially since she'd been taken from this place days before.

"Full circle," Tina said softly as the plane landed.

Drew glanced over at her, his jaw set, his eyes grim.

She wanted to comfort him, but she didn't know how. She was doing the only thing that she could do.

Offer herself up in the deadly game.

When she left the plane, two agents were waiting to meet her. Tina instantly recognized Gunner Ortez and Logan Quinn. Gunner was married to Tina's close friend, Sydney. Normally, Gunner hung back from Tina—from most people, actually. He was the tall, dark and deadly quiet kind of guy. But when he saw Tina leave that tarmac, he pulled her into his arms.

"Nothing will happen to you," he promised against her ear. "If you come out of this mission with so much as a bruise, Syd will have my hide."

A choked laugh escaped her. Tears stung her eyes. "Thank you, Gunner."

His words had been so low that only she could hear them.

"I'll have a lock on you," he told her, pulling back a bit

so he could study her with his steady and determined gaze, "every step of the way."

That was good. She blinked away the tears. Then Tina quickly followed the agents into the hanger. She was wired, hooked up and given a bulletproof vest in mere moments.

She'd worn a bulletproof vest before, during the few times she'd gone into the field. The weight should have reassured her. It didn't.

A knife was slipped into the sheath that had been attached to her ankle. Now she matched Drew. The agents even gave her a gun. Finally.

"They'll probably take the weapons from you as soon as you go inside," Logan Quinn told her. *So much for the gun.* "But they won't be aware of *everything* that you and Drew have."

Because Drew had being loaded down with weapons. Multiple guns. Knives.

She was given backup weapons, too. Now if only she'd had the training to go with them, then she'd be a serious threat.

"Just point and shoot," Logan told her, staring her dead in the eyes. Logan Quinn—Alpha One. He was the team leader of a group of EOD operatives known as the Shadow Agents. In combat, he was lethal. "If they're coming at you, they're coming to kill. You don't hesitate."

Tina nodded. She wished she could have a few minutes alone with Drew.

*Time to tell him goodbye.*

His shoulders were straight. His spine up. Fear had to be twisting through him, but he showed no emotion on his face or in his voice.

He was barking orders. Checking equipment.

How could he be so calm?

"If you don't compartmentalize," Gunner said from her

side, "then you're no good in the field. You have to be able to turn the emotions off."

That was exactly what Drew was doing.

She couldn't do the same. She looked at Drew and she hurt.

She didn't want this for him.

She wanted his family whole. Wanted him happy.

*Because I love him.*

Too fast? Too sudden? She'd known him for several years. Fantasized about him for nearly that whole time. Then when they'd been thrown into close quarters, the reality of the man had far exceeded any of her expectations.

She'd never forget dancing with him in that little room above the Texas bar. He'd let her slide past his guard in those precious moments; she knew that he had.

Logan's phone rang. He stepped aside.

Gunner turned away.

Tina reached for Drew. "I— Can we talk?"

His gaze collided with hers. "I flew you out of this city just nights ago."

She nodded. "I was terrified then."

In that emotionless voice he said, "I was furious. I wanted to destroy those men because they'd hurt you." He paused. "I *did* destroy them."

There was such a dark, dangerous intensity clinging to him. Drew was dressed all in black, and he seemed to be a part of the shadows.

"When I saw you on the rooftop," Tina told him, "I knew that I'd be okay."

His lips thinned. "Stop having so much faith in me."

"I can't." This was the part he needed to understand. "And I need you to have the same faith in me. I won't let you down, Drew. I can do this."

His eyelids flickered. "What if you have another attack?

What if they grab you and put a gun to your head? Are you going to be able to 'do this' when they're ready to shoot a bullet into your brain?"

Tina swallowed. Not such a nice visual. "I'll do anything necessary."

"Now you sound like Mercer." But his hand had lifted. Curled around her shoulder. "I don't want you doing anything necessary. I want you saving lives. I want you *safe.*" He shook his head. "I should have known, though. It seems like everything I touch gets destroyed."

"You don't destroy me." He made her stronger. He made her—

"We've confirmed the location," Logan said as he strode toward them.

Drew's hand tightened.

"We'll make sure there are no civilians nearby," Gunner assured them. "We'll clear the area, damn quietly."

Because if the building exploded, they didn't want civilians getting hurt.

"Time to roll," Logan said.

Tina nodded.

Logan added, "Dylan Foxx is going to meet us on scene. We'll surround the building and make sure we're ready to advance on your command, Drew."

Drew stepped back. He wasn't looking at Logan. His focus seemed to be just for Tina. "You're getting out of this alive, Doc."

Tina grabbed his hands. "So are you."

But he didn't answer her, and a chill encased Tina's heart.

THE TWO-STORY BRICK building waited at the end of the street. A tall, chain-link fence, topped with barbed wire, circled the property.

Four cars were parked outside the building. Two SUVs. Two vans.

One man stood at the main door. Even from a distance, Drew had no trouble seeing the bulge of his weapon.

"Got a man at the back door," Gunner said into Drew's earpiece. "And one canvassing the east side."

"And the west," came Logan's voice. They were all linked, but the transmitter in Drew's ear was so small the enemy shouldn't be able see it, not until it was too late.

Drew climbed from the rental car. He walked around the vehicle and opened Tina's door. When she stepped out, the sunlight glinted off her glasses. Her dark hair brushed over her cheek. She was pale, but her eyes were determined.

She was risking everything for his family.

"Doc, you are the most incredible woman I've ever met."

She blinked and looked a little lost as a furrow appeared between her eyes.

He leaned in close. Put his mouth to her ear. "And I will damn well die before I let them hurt you."

They needed to be clear on that.

His life, not hers.

Never her.

Their hands locked. Together, they approached the building.

The man at the door tensed. He lifted his weapon and aimed it right at Drew.

"I'm Agent Lancaster, and I think you were waiting on me." He paused. "On us. For a trade."

Gunner would have his sites locked on that guy right then. If the fellow moved to fire, all bets were off. Gunner would take him out, and the agents lying in wait around the property would swarm.

But the man didn't fire. Instead, he approached the gate. He fumbled and undid the padlock and let Drew and Tina inside. Then they headed for the door. The wood groaned as it opened. The building was dark and quiet inside.

And Drew could smell blood.

*Paige.*

He didn't rush forward, though. Because his gaze had slid to the left. He saw the bomb that was planted there, just a few feet from the entrance.

"Well, well, well…" a familiar voice called out. "If it isn't…*Stone*…coming back into the family once more."

Hell. Drew focused to the right. The man walking from the shadows had bright blond hair. Angry brown eyes. And a knife in his hand.

*Carl Monroe.*

He'd been hiding just behind one of the bigger parade floats that filled the large warehouse.

"Figured I'd be seeing you again," Carl said. His gaze slid eagerly toward Tina. "I was sure hopin' that I'd be seeing you both again."

"THEY'RE IN THE building," Mercer said as he glared at Anton. He shoved his phone across the table. He'd uncuffed Anton's right wrist. "Now make the call. Get your men on the line. Tell them to release Agent Lancaster's sisters. If those women aren't out in the next sixty seconds…"

Anton laughed and reached for the phone. "I don't care about his sisters. I never did. They were just the means to an end." His eyes narrowed on Mercer. "Your end."

Mercer held his gaze. "Make. The. Call."

Anton punched in numbers. He smirked. The phone was answered on the second ring. "Carl?" Anton said. "Are Lancaster and the girl standing right in front of you?"

Mercer leaned toward Anton.

"Good. Good. Now listen carefully. Let the agent's sisters go.…"

Two men had come up behind Drew and Tina and taken their weapons. Most of them. Drew figured he still had about three blades left on him. They should have done a better job of searching them.

Carl's phone rang. The man answered it, then called out, "Bring the women."

Drew stopped breathing. From the back of the building, he heard the sound of footsteps. Shuffling. Slow. He craned to see, but the floats were in his way. One was a massive green dragon with flames coming from its mouth. Another was a mermaid, her tail crashing into faded blue waves.

But then…then they appeared.

He saw Paige first. Blood trickled down her cheek. So did tears. Helpless to stop himself, he took a step toward her.

And Drew found his own gun shoved at his temple. "That's not the way this works," Carl snapped. One of Carl's hands still held the phone. The other held the gun.

"Tell your sisters that you love them, *Stone,* and then they can walk away."

Kim and Heather were behind Paige. They looked scared, but unharmed.

"Drew?" Paige whispered as more tears slid down her cheeks. "What's happening?" Pretty little Paige. She looked just like their mother. That long, blond hair. The big, blue eyes.

Drew looked like their father. A constant reminder of the man who'd left them. Who'd let them all down.

"You're going to be safe." His voice was cold and flat. The rage was buried as deep inside as it could go. "Just walk out through the front door, go past that fence and you'll be fine."

But Paige shook her head. "You're coming, too?"

No. He wasn't leaving. Not yet.

"The agent doesn't go, honey," Carl cut in. "Not yet."

"I'm not leaving you—" Paige began.

"Then you can die." Carl motioned toward one of his men. The man lifted his gun.

"No!" Tina screamed. "That wasn't the deal. You can't kill them!" She'd rushed toward Drew's sisters. And she put herself right in front of the gun. "Let them go. Let them walk out of here."

Her chest was heaving. Her voice trembling. Fear brightened her eyes and flushed her cheeks.

She was the most beautiful thing Drew had ever seen.

Carl smiled. "Right. You're the one we want…" He waved toward the door. "Go," he said to Paige and the others. "Before you're dead on the floor."

Kim and Heather dragged Paige toward the door. When they crossed the threshold, when they were clear outside, Drew exhaled slowly.

*Alive.*

He knew that Dylan, Gunner and Logan would make sure they stayed that way.

The door closed behind them.

"Now it's your turn," Carl said. He took a step back from Drew. What? The better to aim?

Drew kept his muscles loose. His legs were braced apart, his hands at his sides. He'd attack as soon as the moment was right.

Carl backed up. One step. Another. Then he had his gun at Tina's head.

"All right, boss," Carl said into the phone. "Are you ready for me to pull the trigger?"

ANTON STARED INTO Mercer's eyes. How long had he waited for this moment? And it was everything that he'd hoped it would be.

"Tell your man to stand down," Mercer ordered him.

As if Mercer had the power to give him orders.

"Is the agent still there?" Anton asked softly. "Can he see Tina Jamison very clearly?" Because the agent would need a good, up-close view of what was coming.

"Yes," Carl replied.

Carl. Such a useful man. They both shared a love of pain. This would be a wonderful moment. "Don't pull the trigger, Carl."

He saw Mercer's shoulders relax. Some of the tension slipped from Mercer's face. "I knew you could do the right thing," Mercer said. "I knew—"

*You knew nothing.* "Use your knife on her instead," Anton told him quickly. "Make her hurt, make it last, make her suf—"

"No!" The door to the interrogation room flew open.

Mercer whirled around.

A beautiful blonde stood in the doorway. Her eyes were bright, angry; they were—*Marguerite's eyes.*

"Get out!" Mercer barked at her. A tall, dark-haired man stood just behind the woman. His face was granite-hard. "Agent, I'm giving you an order." Mercer tried to push her away.

The man—the agent—pushed Mercer right back. "She wants to be here. I wasn't going to keep the truth from her."

"Damn it," Mercer swore, his voice a growl. "I told you—"

"I had the wrong woman." Anton barely breathed the words. He couldn't take his gaze off the blonde. He could *see* Marguerite in her.

The sight was almost painful.

Mercer stormed toward Anton. "You're dying. You think

I don't know about the cancer eating you up again? How much time do you have left? Weeks? Days?" He shoved the phone at Anton. "You tell your man to stand down. Tell him not to hurt a hair on Tina Jamison's head."

"She wasn't your daughter." He had to give Mercer credit. He'd outsmarted him damn well. Led him down the wrong trail all along.

The blonde came fully into the interrogation room. Her guard—the agent had to be her bodyguard—shut the door behind her.

"I'm Mercer's daughter. The woman you're trying to kill just got caught in the cross fire." Her gaze was steady, direct. "She's not of any use to you now. Let her go."

"Boss? *Boss?*" Carl demanded, his voice cracking from the phone.

"I won't be able to kill you," Anton said as he realized the truth. There just wasn't enough time left. "But it's okay. I wanted him to suffer, as I suffered…" He forced his gaze off Marguerite.

*No, she's not Marguerite.*

He didn't know her name. Right then, he didn't want to know.

"You will suffer, Mercer, because that woman down in New Orleans might not be your blood, but I heard the emotion in your voice when you talked to her. Sometimes, it's not just blood that makes a family, is it?" He didn't even feel the pain in his chest anymore. The pain that had eaten at him for so long. This was his moment. "Go ahead, Carl," he ordered as he raised his voice so the man would hear him. "Kill her."

"No!" the blonde screamed.

She was too late.

There was no going back now.

CARL SMILED. He tossed aside his phone. "I've got my orders. She's gonna die. I'll cut her, again and again, and she's gonna scream for me."

Tina wasn't making a sound right then.

"The hell she is," Drew snarled at the bastard.

Footsteps shuffled behind him. He tensed. Two men, armed. Were they coming to kill him? *Let's see you try.*

"They can take you outside," Carl said, surprising him, "or you can die right here with her."

Why were they trying to make him leave? That didn't make sense. Anton Devast was a sadistic freak. He would want to take out everyone in his path.

*So why free my sisters? Why try to let me go?*

This scene wasn't adding up to Drew.

Rough hands grabbed his arms and hauled him back.

Tina still wasn't speaking. She was just watching him with those wide, resolute eyes of hers.

That knife was so close to her throat. If he fought the two men right then, in front of Carl, the SOB could slit her throat while he watched.

No, he couldn't risk it. He had to pick a better moment to attack. *Hold on, Tina. I'll get you out of here.*

That was what he tried to tell her with his stare, but what he said was, "Goodbye, Doc."

She blinked back tears.

They pulled him away. Shoved him toward the door.

When he tried to turn back, the taller man put a gun to Drew's head. "Now walk away, hero. Don't look back. Just go."

Was Carl already using his blade on Tina? He didn't hear a sound coming from her.

"There's going to be no escape for you two," Drew said, deliberately using the code word because he wanted the

EOD agents to swarm. "You won't be able to just walk out of here. You have to know that's not going to happen."

But the men just smirked at him. "Who said anything about walking?"

Drew was directly in front of the main entrance. A few more steps and he'd be out of the building.

Only, he didn't plan to leave.

"Why just follow orders?" he demanded even as he palmed the small blade he'd tucked beneath his belt. *You missed that one on your weapons search.* "Why let Devast use you? He's going to make sure you all die, too. Don't you realize that?"

But the men started laughing. Drew's hold on his weapon tightened.

"You don't really think we're letting you all go, do you?" the taller guy demanded.

"Ten, nine, eight…" his sidekick began.

Drew tensed. "What the—?"

"Your sisters were wired, *Agent* Lancaster. Hell, I don't think they even knew those collars we snapped around their necks were set to blow—"

Drew spun for the door. He rushed outside.

"The EOD agents got them, right? Those guys who are surrounding us? Guess they'll all go boom soon enough."

*"Three…two…"*

An explosion erupted, shaking the ground and sending Drew flying.

TINA SCREAMED WHEN she heard the explosion.

The knife sliced the side of her neck.

"That will keep those agents busy." Carl smiled at her. "I'm supposed to take my time with you, so let's go, honey. Let's go enjoy ourselves."

More men rushed inside. They all headed to the back of the building. Carl was trying to haul her that way, too.

More explosions erupted, only this time they were *in* the building. The detonations seemed to come one right after the other. Devast's men were destroying everything—and making it impossible for anyone to follow them as they fled through the float graveyard.

Chunks of the old floats flew into the air. A dragon's papier-mâché head ignited a few feet from her.

"You think Devast didn't plan this end?" Carl jerked her head back with a painful grip on her hair. "He made sure we could escape—and that we'd take you with us. Mercer will be getting pieces of you sent to him for weeks."

They were sick. "I'm not…going…" The smoke was rising. Filling her lungs.

*Breathe.*

They'd taken her inhaler. When they'd searched her at the door, they'd taken her weapons and her medicine.

The smoke made her eyes burn. The flames heated her skin.

The men kicked open the back door. Fresh air blew inside and she tried to take deep, greedy gulps.

But then gunfire erupted. The *rat-a-tat* sent the men scrambling back inside the building. Tina tried to duck for cover, but Carl wasn't letting her go.

The back door swung open. A man raced inside. His blond hair gleamed in the faint light. He wore black, and she could see the bulky outline of his bulletproof vest. He had a gun in each hand, and his bullets hit with deadly accuracy, slamming into the men who'd thought they'd had an easy escape.

With the EOD, nothing was ever easy. Devast had underestimated his opponents.

"Stop!" Carl yelled. Tina was in front of him. His human shield. "Throw down your weapons and get back or she *dies!*"

But the man shook his head. He lifted his guns. Seemed to be aiming—

*At me?* Yes, he was.

"You aren't getting away. The EOD doesn't negotiate with terrorists." She didn't recognize the agent's unaccented voice, but she sure recognized Mercer's familiar line.

*He's going to shoot me.* To take out Carl, she realized the agent would need to get rid of Carl's protection. Tina braced for the pain.

Before another gunshot erupted, someone slammed into them. She and Carl both hit the ground with an impact hard enough to crack bones. Tina was pretty sure she *did* hear one of Carl's bones break, and that savage sound made her heart race faster. The knife had sliced over her collarbone when she fell, and more blood soaked her shirt as Tina rolled away from her attacker.

She pushed up to her knees and saw—

*Drew.*

He'd come back. She'd known that he would. Happiness and hope fought inside her.

But…his expression was brutal. Wild. He was driving his fist into Carl's face again and again.

Carl's head slammed into the concrete, and he stopped moving.

"Come on!" It was the EOD agent. The one she didn't know. He was grabbing her arms and pulling her up to her feet. "My orders are to get you out of here!"

The flames were spreading. Would more bombs be detonating soon?

"The whole place is going to blow—it's their distraction. They thought they'd get away while the whole block burned."

His hold on her wrist was unbreakable.

Drew rose to his feet.

Tina tried to reach for him. "Drew! Come on!"

He looked up at her.

Her heart stopped.

Something was...wrong. Drew's eyes looked dead. His face was a mask of fury and rage—but his eyes were *dead*.

"Drew?"

Another detonation shook the building. Cracks ran across the remaining walls and chunks of the ceiling fell, narrowly missing them.

"They were timed to start right after Lancaster went out the door," the agent shouted. "Come on, we have to *move*."

Wait, Drew had gone out and then come back through that hell? He'd walked back into the flames?

Her breath heaved out as she fought to break the mysterious agent's hold and get back to Drew.

But the agent wasn't letting her go.

"Drew!" He seemed frozen. He needed to move.

Because Carl was moving again. Carl had just grabbed the knife from the floor. He wasn't unconscious; he'd just been waiting for his moment to attack. He lunged up and went straight for Drew's back.

"Behind you!" Tina screamed. The fire was crackling so loudly she wasn't sure he even heard her. "Drew!"

At the last moment he spun around. He grabbed Carl's hand, stopping that knife before it could shove into his body.

Drew twisted Carl's hand. Carl howled—she could hear the stark cry of pain rising over the flames—then Drew plunged the knife into Carl's chest.

This time, when he hit the ground, Carl wasn't pretending to be unconscious. He was dead.

"Have to do this..." the agent muttered as Tina kept struggling against him. She needed to get to Drew. "Orders..."

Forget orders.

Drew looked up then, staring at her with the eyes that weren't his.

He shook his head, as if waking up, then he ran toward her. Tina stopped fighting the other agent. She ran with him—and Drew.

The smoke was choking her, her lungs were burning, but she wasn't about to let the attack stop her. Not now, not when they were home free.

The fresh air was just steps away.

Steps—

"Bomb!" Drew yelled. "Above the back door. The timer's counting down—"

She could see it. The seconds were showing in a digital red flash. They only had four seconds. *Four.*

They raced outside. She couldn't pull in any breath. Her legs just kept going. *Escape.* That had been their code word. She just needed to—

When the last bomb detonated, the force tossed Tina as if she were a rag doll.

# Chapter Eleven

Anton Devast inclined his head. "And then there was nothing left." He'd been watching the clock on the stark, white interrogation room wall. If Carl had followed his orders, if he'd stayed on the schedule Devast had made for the detonations, then the float graveyard had just blown up in New Orleans.

The whole block would be a wreck.

His chaos. His havoc.

Mercer had his phone out. He was pulling the pretty blonde from the room. Demanding to know the status—

The door shut behind Mercer.

Anton exhaled slowly. It wasn't the revenge he'd wanted.

But it would have to do.

"Tina!"

Drew wiped the blood from his eye as he leaped to his feet. His clothes were singed, blisters covered his arms and— *Where was Tina?*

She'd been in front of him before the last detonation. He'd tried to reach for her, but the blast had torn her away from him.

His gaze searched to the left. The right. Smoke billowed all around him. Tina couldn't stay in this smoke. It would hurt her.

Maybe that's why she wasn't calling back to him. Maybe she was having another attack. The smoke had set it off before, on that runway, and maybe—

"D-Drew…" Just a whisper; a strangled gasp that he heard above the flames.

That gasp was the sweetest sound to his ears. It meant that she was alive.

He ran to her, following that gasp. She was on the ground, struggling to sit up. He shoved his hand into the hidden pocket on his vest and pulled out her inhaler. "Easy, Doc, I've got you."

*Always.*

She took the inhaler. Her lashes lifted so that her eyes met his.

The fire was still spreading, surging higher and higher. Sirens wailed in the distance.

"I have to get you out of here." He scooped her up into his arms. It wasn't about a mission or priorities. He didn't think it ever had been. It was only about her.

Now, she truly was the only good thing left in his life.

He looked up. The other agent was there—the man who'd come up behind the building and taken out most of Devast's men. Cooper Marshall. Drew knew the guy by reputation, but had never worked with him. Cooper's blond hair stuck to his temples, slick with sweat. He had a gun in his left hand. "Get her out," Cooper barked. "I'll make sure we're clear."

And that no more of Devast's men had survived to attack again.

Drew held tight to Tina as he raced away from the scene. He'd gotten her out of that inferno. She was in his arms. *Safe.*

When he'd learned about his sisters—

*No.*

Drew immediately slammed the door on that thought. *Not now. Can't think of them now.* He was barely holding together as it was.

He had to protect Tina first.

Tina, then—

*Paige had wanted to stay with me.*

His back teeth ground together. His eyes burned.

His arms clung even harder to Tina. He kept running with her cradled against him. The smoke was so thick that he could barely see as he rushed forward.

She had her medicine. She was safe. Alive.

His sisters…

*I'm so sorry.* He'd failed them. Let them all down. They'd died, because of him.

The sirens were wailing. He could see the lights of an ambulance approaching.

Grief threatened to choke him, but Drew kept running toward that ambulance.

Police were on the scene now. Drew caught sight of Gunner and Logan. They were keeping the local authorities back.

They'd all have to stay back until they made sure there weren't any more bombs. The rescue teams would be held in a safe zone until the bomb squad completed their sweeps.

He had to make it to that zone.

Just a few more steps…

*Made it.*

The EMTs reached for Tina. They put her on a stretcher. She shoved their hands back. "Drew—"

"You're safe." Ash stained the hand that he slid over her cheek. "It's over."

His heart was leaden in his chest. His whole body seemed numb. He'd used his control in the field more times than he could count; locking his emotions away. But this was different—

*My family is gone.*

Tina grabbed his hand when he would have stepped back. "Wh-what…h-happened?"

The EMTs were trying to work on her, but she kept pushing them away and clinging to Drew.

"Your eyes…" Tina whispered. "They're wrong…some-thing…happened."

He didn't know what she meant about his eyes. Other than the fact that they kept burning as if they were on fire. Drew shook his head.

"T-tell me…"

His shoulders bowed. "They killed my sisters…" He should have known the exchange was too easy. His dark-ness, his job—it had cost Kim, Heather and Paige their lives.

"Drew!"

His head whipped up at that frantic call. That had—had just sounded like Paige.

"I can…see them," Tina said, voice husky. Her gaze slid over Drew's shoulder. "Not…dead."

He spun around.

Walking through the smoke, he saw Dylan—and his friend was right beside Paige, Kim and Heather.

*Alive.* All of them were *alive!*

Drew shook his head. No, no, the explosion—

Paige ran to him. She hit his chest so hard that he took a step back. She was crying and laughing and holding on to him as tightly as she could.

Drew's stunned gaze rose and met Dylan's.

"Devast used devices like those collars two years ago, back in Brazil." Dylan's lashes flickered. "Those vics didn't get free in time. I wasn't going to let the same thing happen again."

Then Kim and Heather were there. All holding him. All laughing and crying as the smoke drifted in the air.

The ambulance's siren wailed once more. He looked back. The ambulance's door had just slammed.

The EMTs were taking Tina away.

He tried to head toward the ambulance, but his sisters tightened their hold on him.

Drew needed to make them understand. "I have to—"

"I thought we were all going to die," Paige whispered as the tears slid silently down her cheeks. "Is this…is this what you do?"

"You risk your life like this, all the time?" Heather's face was stark, white. Fear lit her eyes.

He couldn't answer her. Families weren't supposed to know about the missions he faced.

Families also weren't supposed to be pulled into his battles.

"I'm sorry," he said, the words rough and rumbling from deep in his throat.

Dylan pressed his hand to Kim's shoulder. "We need to get you ladies to the hospital. We want you all checked out."

And the scene wasn't safe.

Tina's ambulance had left.

Another ambulance was waiting, its back doors open. The EMTs came forward to help his sisters.

Drew caught Dylan's arm. "Thank you."

Dylan inclined his head. "Man, you should know I always have your back."

He did.

The flames were burning, raging so brightly behind them. More havoc.

The group's name had come from the destruction they left behind.

Destruction and death.

Only this time there had been survivors, too. Innocent lives had been saved.

Devast wouldn't hurt anyone else.

*No, you bastard, you didn't know my price.*

And Devast never would.


SWEET OXYGEN FLOWED into Tina's lungs. The ambulance rolled and bounced as it raced from the scene.

Drew's sisters had been hugging him.

She swallowed.

They'd made it out alive. The mission was finally over.

Now it was time for her to go back to the life that waited for her.

Time for him to return to his life. His missions.

They'd see each other at the EOD.

She'd remember. How could she ever forget what they'd shared?

"Miss? Miss…are you hurting?"

A tear had dropped down her cheek. Tina shook her head. There wasn't anything the medics could do for the pain that she felt.


"WHERE THE HELL IS SHE?" Drew demanded as he slammed his hands down on the nurses' station desk.

"Sir, you need to calm down."

"What I need is to find the patient who was brought in! Dr. Tina Jamison! She came in by ambulance two hours ago."

Two of the longest hours of his life. He'd stayed on scene, needing to make sure the last arm of HAVOC was truly destroyed. He'd gone in on the bomb sweeps, checked all the nearby buildings to make sure they also weren't set to blow.

They'd used the bomb-sniffing dogs. Gone in and out—searching every possible area. They'd found two more bombs.

The bomb squad had disarmed them with seconds to spare.

Sweat coated Drew's body as he glared at the nurse in front of him. He'd been through hell, and he needed to see his damn angel. "Where is she?"

"We have no record of a Tina Jamison, sir. She didn't come in here. You must have the wrong hospital."

No, he didn't, and Drew was perilously close to tearing the place apart with his bare hands.

"They took her back to Dallas."

He stiffened at Gunner's voice. Drew glanced over his shoulder.

Gunner inclined his head to the right. "Come with me."

If Gunner was giving him information on Tina, then he'd go anyplace with the guy. His steps hurried, Drew followed Gunner to a quiet corner and, once he was sure no one could overhear him, he squared off against the sharpshooter. "Why wasn't I told about her transfer?"

"Because you were still on scene, defusing bombs." Gunner lifted a dark brow. "Your lady is all right. You can rest easy on that. Tina was stable when she boarded the flight."

*Your lady...* Gunner had always been observant. Drew nodded and tried to calm his racing heart. "You saw her then?"

"I did. Cooper was with her. Hell..." He ran a weary hand over his face as he muttered, "That guy is a ghost. I didn't even know he was working the Devast case until I saw him jump in the ambulance with her on scene."

Cooper had been in the ambulance?

"Seems Mercer gave him orders. Protect Dr. Jamison at all costs."

Drew stiffened. "Mercer didn't think I could do the job?"

Gunner's gaze was steady. "Mercer knows that when emotions get involved, even good agents can get compromised."

"I wouldn't have traded her safety for *anything*. I was going back in after her—"

"You dying for her wouldn't have saved her life. And we both know that was exactly what you planned to do." Flat, cold words.

True words. He would have traded his life for Tina in an instant. Drew didn't look away from Gunner's direct stare.

"Does she know?" Gunner asked quietly.

He had to get on a flight to Dallas. "Know what?"

Gunner laughed. The sound caught Drew off guard. As far as he knew, the guy never laughed.

But then, as far as the rest of the agents seemed to be concerned, Drew didn't feel, either.

*Ice in my veins.*

No, he had fire in his veins right then.

"Why don't you take some friendly advice from someone who's been where you are…?" Gunner's lips twisted in a wry smile. "Don't just stand back and let the thing you want the most slip away from you."

The fire burned ever hotter inside him. "But what if I'm not right for her? She needs someone—"

"Let her decide what she needs. Who she needs. Go for what *you* want." Then Gunner turned away from him. "I'm going home. My wife is waiting for me."

His wife. His very pregnant wife. Gunner had a wife who loved him—and twins on the way.

"How did you—?" Drew stopped.

Gunner glanced back at him.

"Weren't you afraid? That what we do… Weren't you scared that it would spill over on them?"

But, no, Gunner's wife, Sydney, she was part of the EOD. She'd worked for years in the field. She knew all about danger. "Never mind," Drew said, shaking his head. "I shouldn't have—"

"I was more afraid," Gunner admitted, voice low, "of trying to live my life without her."

Drew thought of his life. The missions. One after the other. Coming home.

Being alone.

He'd looked forward to his visits to the EOD office— *because I knew I would see Tina.*

Is that what he wanted to happen? Would he return to only seeing Tina every few months? He'd keep his emotions sealed off and try to go on with his life without her?

He'd watch life from the outside? Day in and day out, he'd long for what he couldn't have.

*I told her there would be no going back.* Because he didn't want to go back to a life that didn't involve Tina. He needed her far too much.

He walked down the corridor. His sisters were in a private room. Police guards made sure they weren't disturbed.

Paige had gotten stitches. Kim and Heather had been bruised, but otherwise unharmed. They'd been very, very lucky.

He stepped into the room with them. Shut the door behind him.

No one spoke at first. Drew realized that he didn't know what to say.

He hadn't been in a room with the three of them since—

"I miss you," Paige told him. A bandage was on her neck. On her arm. White bandages against her skin.

"We all miss you," Kim added in a soft tone.

Drew swallowed. *No ice.*

"Why don't you ever come home?" Heather asked him.

He didn't have a home. Not anymore.

Paige walked toward him. The baby. The kid sister. Did she know that he'd kept every letter she'd ever sent him?

"My life…" He stopped, cleared his throat and tried again. "I never wanted it to hurt you."

But it had. Their worlds had collided. "It was my fault that you were hurt. A very…dangerous man tracked the money I'd been sending to you."

Paige stood in front of him. "Is he going to come after us again?"

Drew shook his head.

Her pale lips curved. "We don't want your money, Drew. We just want you."

And he wanted them. He wanted his family back.

He wanted a *life*.

Not ice.

Maybe it was time to take the risk—and to take what he wanted most.


TINA WALKED SLOWLY down the hallway of the FBI's office in Dallas. Cooper Marshall was at her side. The guy seemed to be her constant shadow.

She was his mission—at least, for about five more feet, she was.

Tina stopped in front of Mercer's temporary headquarters. He'd commandeered the biggest office in the place. Figured. That was Mercer. Always making friends left and right.

"Thanks, Agent Marshall," Tina said. "I'm here, safe and sound."

Cooper inclined his head toward her. He didn't talk much. The agent sure seemed to be the quiet and intense type.

Once, Tina would have described Drew the exact same way. Except—

He seemed to talk plenty when they were together.

*We aren't together any longer. The mission is over. So are we.*

The door opened. Mercer stood there. "Dr. Jamison, come in..."

She stepped across the threshold.

Cooper started to follow.

"Sorry, son," Mercer said, sounding not the least bit actually sorry as he held up his hand to block Cooper, "but you don't have clearance for this."

Then he shut the door in Cooper's surprised face.

Tina took a few tentative steps inside the office. She glanced around the room and she instantly realized just why Cooper didn't have clearance.

Two other people were waiting in that office.

She knew the EOD Agent, Cale Lane. She'd patched him up a few times. And the other woman—the woman with the blond hair and the perfect face—that was Cassidy Sherridan.

Well...technically she was Cassidy Sherridan *Lane* now.

The blonde was Mercer's real daughter.

She was also rushing across the room and *hugging* Tina. "I'm so sorry," Cassidy told her, squeezing her tightly. "As soon as I found out, I came right away. I told Anton who I was."

"And I damn well told *you* to keep her away," Mercer growled to Cale.

"I'm not lying to my wife." Cale was resolute. Determined. Protective.

Cassidy pulled back a bit to study Tina. "I can't ever make this up to you."

Tina frowned at her and shook her head. "There's nothing to make up. You didn't do anything to me. It was all Anton." She glanced toward Mercer. His arms were crossed over his chest, but his gaze was on her—and it was worried. "Is his network contained? Is it over?"

"Yes."

Her shoulders slumped. "Then we saved lives. The risk was worth it."

"But you shouldn't have been risked," Cassidy whispered as she stepped back. "You should never have been in harm's way."

Tina had to smile at that. "And you should have been? We can't help who we are...or who we're not." She felt... different standing in that room with Mercer and Cassidy. Before the nightmare of her abduction, Tina had always been a bit in awe of Mercer and all the EOD agents.

And she'd been...afraid. Of so much. Of letting her weakness hurt others. Of being caught in the cross fire once more.

"I'm not weak," Tina said.

Mercer's eyes narrowed.

Cale stood beside Cassidy.

"Who the hell said you were?" Now anger lit Mercer's eyes. "If Lancaster—"

Tina shook her head. "I'm the one who thought it. Drew never said anything." She pushed her glasses—another replacement pair because she'd lost the others in the blast down in New Orleans—up a bit on her nose. "I've been hiding for a long time, and I don't want to do that anymore." She *wouldn't* stay in her labs. Wouldn't live through the actions of others.

It was time for her to seize her own adventures.

Only, maybe these new adventures wouldn't involve death and destruction.

"You let me hide," she said to Mercer because she'd seen through his mask.

His jaw hardened. "I wanted you safe."

Cassidy laughed softly. Sympathy flashed across her face. "Oh, Mercer…when you keep us safe, sometimes you keep us caged."

Tina didn't want to be caged anymore. Not by Mercer and not by her own fear.

The past couldn't haunt her, and she wouldn't spend her days afraid of what might come.

Mercer stared into Tina's eyes. "What about Lancaster?"

He always saw so much. "He did his job. It's over now."

There had never been any talk of a future from him. Never any talk of emotions.

Tina knew what she felt, but as for Drew…

*Maybe I couldn't ever get past the ice.*

It sure had felt as if she had, though. His torch had seemed to scorch right to her very soul.

Frantic pounding sounded on the door.

Mercer jerked his head. Cale immediately reached for Cassidy, and they slipped out a side door.

*No wonder Mercer picked this office.*

When they were clear, Mercer yanked open the main door. "I'm in a private meeting, what do you want?"

Cooper stood to the side. Two FBI agents—decked out in pressed suits—stared at Mercer with wide eyes.

"The prisoner is seizing, sir. We've called medical personnel but—"

"It could be a trick," Mercer snarled as he rushed past them.

Tina was right on his heels. There was only one "prisoner" who would have sparked this kind of reaction from Mercer.

They zigged and zagged through the halls. Then they were entering a small room that she hadn't seen before. No windows. Only one narrow door to gain entry into that place.

Anton Devast lay slumped on a narrow cot in the room. Two agents were with him, trying to turn his head so that he could breathe.

Anton's eyes widened when he caught sight of her. "Dead…"

No, she wasn't.

Tina fell to her knees next to him. His breath was jerking out, his heart—beating too slowly.

She stared at his skin, noting the blue tinges and the sunken lines around his eyes and mouth.

He tried to lift his hand to reach for her.

But he didn't have the strength.

His eyes flared. His lips trembled as he tried to speak. Only, he couldn't talk anymore. It was too late.

Anton Devast was still staring at Tina when he died.

IT WAS BACK to business as usual at the EOD.

Tina stepped into her lab, the white lab coat she wore a familiar comfort to her. After Devast's death, she'd been caught up in a whirlwind. A whirlwind controlled by Mercer. Before she'd barely blinked, she'd found herself back in D.C.

With, of course, Agent Cooper Marshall at her side.

She hadn't seen Drew again. Hadn't heard from him.

His sisters were safe, alive— She carried the image of them embracing him in her mind.

But Drew...he just seemed to be gone.

Had he already taken another mission? Gone out on another undercover assignment? Was he in the U.S.? Already halfway around the world?

She didn't know.

But Tina would find out.

Her hair was twisted into a small bun and her steps were sure as she searched around her lab. *Less than a week.* How could one life change so quickly?

Hers had, irrevocably, and there was no going back now.

She realized the full meaning of Drew's warning to her. When he'd said there would be no going back, she should have paid more attention. Her old life had vanished, destroyed in the heat of their passion.

Her new life seemed too cold. Too sterile and stark, without him.

*I miss him.*

The door squeaked open behind her.

"Be with you in a second," she said, throwing the words over her shoulder as she bent to peer into the low cabinet.

"Take your time," a slow, drawling voice told her, the smallest hint of Mississippi deepening those words. "I'm not going anywhere."

*Drew.*

She straightened slowly, then turned toward him. He stood just inside the doorway, his shoulder propped against the door frame. His eyes were on her.

And he was staring at her as if he could eat her alive.

Only fair, she was probably ogling him the same way.

"I missed you in New Orleans." He stepped away from the door. Locked it. "And in Dallas." He stalked toward her.

"Mercer wanted me to come back—"

"I'm not real interested in what Mercer wants."

Neither was she. Her gaze slid over him. Tall. Dark. Deadly. That was Drew. But his eyes—they were bright.

They seemed to shine with emotion.

But Tina didn't know if she could trust what she was seeing in his gaze.

"Don't." He stopped in front of her.

"Don't what?" Why was her voice so husky?

"That's not the way you usually look at me."

She swallowed, not sure what he was talking about.

"Usually, you stare at me with trust. I look into your eyes, and I want to be the man you think I am."

He was.

She made herself ask, "How am I looking at you now?"

"Like you've lost faith in me." The faint lines near his mouth deepened. "Doc, *don't*. I've been tracking you. I've been steps behind you all the way home."

"I—I thought you might be on another mission."

He nodded. "I am. The most important mission of my life."

Oh, right. Now she understood. Another mission meant he had to be medically cleared for the field. She cleared her throat. "In light of what's…happened…another doctor here can—"

"I don't want another doctor." His hands wrapped around her waist and he lifted her up. He sat her on the exam table. Put them eye-to-eye and leaned in real close to her. "You're the one I want. The *only* one I want."

"Drew—"

He kissed her.

Kissed her with passion, with need, with raw lust.

Kissed her as if he were desperate.

Kissed her as if she were his life.

She kissed him back just as fiercely. Her arms curled around his neck and she pulled him tightly to her.

She didn't care where they were. She had him in her arms again, and she'd take this moment while she could.

It was her new philosophy. Grab life. Hold on tight.

She was sure holding tight to him.

When he licked her bottom lip, a delicious shudder slid over her.

"I love you."

It took a minute for his growled words to sink in. When they did, Tina shook her head.

He pulled back, just a few inches, and his golden stare held hers. "I. Love. You."

"You don't have to say—"

"The truth? Yeah, Doc, I do." He brushed back a lock of hair that had escaped from her bun. "I wanted to tell you in New Orleans. I wanted to tell you in Dallas. Hell, I even wanted to tell you in Lightning."

What? No, he could not have just said that.

"I haven't loved another woman, haven't gotten close to anyone, the way I have with you." His fingers curled under her jaw. "You slipped right past my walls. Made me want things…things I never thought I *could* have."

If this was a dream, she had better not ever wake up. "You can have anything."

He smiled at her. "You're what I want."

Her tall, dark and deadly agent was staring straight at her—and looking at Tina as if she was his world.

"I know you don't love me," he said, and he spoke those words with a determined pride that made her heart ache, "but give me a chance. That's all I'm asking for. A chance to show you that we can be good together. No bombs. No danger. No threats. Just you and me. Give me the time to—"

"No." That one word sent silence through the room.

His hand slid away from her. He swallowed. The soft sound was almost painful to hear. "Then I won't push you anymore. I'm sorry. I—I guess I should have let you go."

*Never.*

She grabbed his arm when he tried to ease away. The new stitches that she had on her neck—courtesy of that jerk Carl—pulled a bit. Tina ignored the little flash of pain. Some things were more important than pain. "I don't need to take any kind of chance on you. I *know* that I love you."

He blinked at her.

Ah, so she'd finally caught her agent by surprise. Only fair. He'd sure broken into her world and turned everything upside down.

"I loved you in New Orleans," she told him softly. His pupils widened. The darkness fought the gold of his eyes. "I loved you in Dallas." She smiled at him and hoped that he could see the emotion in her eyes. "And I loved you in Lightning." She'd tried to tell him, to show him, in a million small ways.

Tina leaned forward and brushed her lips over his. She reached around him, her hands sliding over his coat.

She frowned when she felt the small bulge in his pocket.

Her brows lifted as her fingers slid inside that pocket. She touched the familiar form of an inhaler.

"I want you to always be safe," he whispered. "I want you close to me, and I want to make sure I can help you."

"You've been carrying this—"

"Since I found out what you needed. I want to be the man you need. The man who makes you smile in the morning." A wicked glint lit his eyes. "The man who makes you moan at night."

"You are." Her heart was beating faster—because she was happy. The happiest she'd been in years.

It wasn't about taking a chance on him. Wasn't about the unknown risk of falling for a dangerous agent.

It was about what the heart wanted.

About trust.

About love.

"My sisters want to meet you," he said as his lips lowered toward hers. "They want to meet the woman who saved them."

"But I didn't—"

"Yes, you did. Doc, you're the bravest, strongest woman I've ever met. And I don't know how I got so lucky as to find you, but I don't ever want to let you go."

She tilted her head back. "You don't have to let me go." Fair warning time. "Because I'm not going to let you go."

"Forever?" Hope was there, in his eyes. Hope and love and happiness.

In his eyes. In his voice. On his face.

"Forever," Tina promised. She kissed him and knew that she'd found the right man. The only man for her.

# Epilogue

Bruce Mercer gazed down at the busy Washington, D.C., streets below his office. The sidewalks were full of people, and cars bustled on the pavement.

Those people lived their whole lives without realizing the danger that truly stalked the world. The danger his agents faced every single day.

"The last case was too close," he said quietly. He'd almost lost Tina, *and* Cassidy's true identity had nearly come to light.

Good thing only a dead man had heard Cassidy's confession.

Devast had gotten intel that the man *never* should have possessed. The EOD tracking devices had been designed to protect the agents.

Not put them at increased risk.

Devast was dead, but the case wasn't over. Not completely. There was a traitor in the EOD. Someone in his organization was selling out agents who were already risking their lives.

That traitor would have to be stopped.

Mercer turned away from the busy street and gazed at the agent who sat, silent and still, in the leather chair. "It was close, but you did a good job on this mission, Agent Marshall."

Cooper Marshall inclined his head.

"Now I've got another case for you." Bruce stalked slowly toward him. "I want you to find my traitor, and I want you to stop him."

Cooper gazed up at him for a moment. "You're sure it's one of our own?"

"Yes." And that just made the betrayal even harder to take. "Trust no one on this case, Marshall. A man—or woman—who will sell out his own teammates—that person will be the most dangerous enemy you've ever faced."

And that enemy was *in* the EOD. He or she could be walking through the offices right then.

Mercer had thought he'd already cleaned house at the EOD. Every employee there *should* have been carefully screened.

But he'd messed up. He'd trusted the wrong person, and now his agents were paying for his mistake.

*They can't pay with their lives.*

"Stop the traitor," Mercer ordered him again. "By any means necessary."

* * * * *

*Read on for a special sneak peek of*
*THE GIRL NEXT DOOR,*
*the next installment of the*
**SHADOW AGENTS: GUTS & GLORY** *miniseries,*
*coming from Intrigue March 2014!*

# Chapter One

Cooper Marshall burst into the apartment, his gun ready even as his gaze swept the dim interior of the room that waited for him. "Lockwood!"

There was no response to his call, but the stench in the air—that unmistakable odor of death and blood—told Cooper he'd arrived too late.

Again.

*Damn it.*

He'd gotten his orders from the top. He'd been assigned to track down Keith Lockwood, an ex-Elite Operations Division agent. Cooper was supposed to confirm that the other man was alive and well. He'd fallen off the EOD's radar, and that had sure raised a red flag in the mind of Cooper's boss.

Especially since other EOD agents had recently turned up dead.

Cooper rounded a corner in the narrow hallway. The scent of blood was stronger. He headed toward what he suspected was the bedroom. His eyes had already adjusted to the darkness, so it was easy for him to see the body slumped on the floor just a few feet from him.

He knelt, and his gloved fingers turned the body just slightly. Cooper pulled out his penlight and shone it on the dead man's face.

Keith Lockwood. Cooper had never worked with the man on a mission, but he'd seen Lockwood's photos.

Lockwood's throat had been slit. An up-close kill.

Considering that Lockwood was a former navy SEAL, the man shouldn't have been caught off guard.

But he had been.

*Because the killer isn't your average thug off the streets.*

The killer was also an agent with the EOD, and the killer was trained just as well as Lockwood had been.

No, trained *better*.

Because the killer had been able to get the drop on the SEAL.

Cooper's breath eased out in a rough sigh just as a knock sounded on the front door.

The front door that Cooper had just smashed open moments before.

He leaped to his feet.

"Mr. Lockwood?" a feminine voice called out. "Mr. Lockwood…i-is everything all right?"

No, things were far from *all right*. The broken door *should* have been a dead giveaway on that point.

"It's Gabrielle Harper!" the voice continued. "We were supposed to meet…"

His back teeth clenched. Talk about extremely bad timing. He knew Gabrielle Harper, and the trouble the woman was about to bring his way just was going to make the situation even more of a tangled mess.

Cooper holstered his weapon. He had to get out of that apartment. *Before* Gabrielle saw him and asked questions he couldn't answer for her.

He rose and stalked toward the bedroom window. His footsteps were silent. After all of his training, they should be.

Gabrielle's steps—and her high heels—tapped across the hardwood floor as she came inside the apartment.

*Of course,* Gabrielle wasn't just going to wait outside. She was a reporter, no doubt on the scent of a story.

*And she must have scented the blood.*

She was following that scent, and if he didn't move, fast, she'd follow it straight to him.

Cooper opened the window, then glanced down below. Three floors up. But there were bricks on the side of the building, with crevices in between them. If he held on just right, he could spider crawl his way down.

The floor in the hallway creaked as Gabrielle paused.

*She should have called for help by now.* At the first sign of that smashed door, Gabrielle should have dialed 9-1-1. But, with Gabrielle, what she *should* do and what she actually *did*—well, those could be very different things.

If she wasn't careful, the woman was going to walk into real danger one day. The kind she wouldn't be able to walk away from.

He slid through the window. Since it was after midnight, Cooper knew he'd be able to blend pretty easily with the darkness when he climbed down the backside of the building.

He'd make it out of there, undetected, provided he didn't fall and break his neck.

He eased to the side, his feet resting against the window's narrow ledge. He pulled the window back down and took a deep breath.

"*Mr. Lockwood!*" Gabrielle's horror-filled scream broke loud and clearly through the night.

She'd found the body.

Jaw locking, Cooper made his way down the building.

Gabrielle had just stumbled into an extremely dangerous situation. Now he'd have to do some serious recon to keep her out of the cross fire.

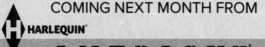

## THE SECRET OF CHEROKEE COVE
### by Paula Graves

*Dana Massey's life is turned upside down, by both a family secret and the offer of protection by the very sexy detective Walter Nix.*

"What do you know about the Cumberlands?"

His back stiffened for a second at the sound of the name, and he shot Dana a quick look.

"Why do you ask?" he said.

"My mother's maiden name was Tallie Cumberland. Ever heard of her?"

Dread ran through him like ice in his blood, freezing him as if he was still that little boy from Cherokee Cove who believed every tale his mama told him, especially the scary ones.

"You *have* heard of her."

"I've heard of the Cumberlands."

"Doyle says the most anyone would tell him is that the Cumberlands are nothing but trouble."

"Does that sound anything like your mother?" he asked carefully.

"No."

"Then I wouldn't worry about it."

Dana didn't say anything else until they reached the Bitterwood city limits. Even then, she merely said she'd told Doyle she was going to stay at his house.

"Are you sure you feel safe there?"

"I'm armed, and I'm too wired to sleep."

HIEXP69746

"I could stick around."

"And protect the poor, defenseless girl?"

"Not what I said."

"I'm usually not this prickly. It's been an unsettling night."

"I'm serious about sticking around. Couldn't hurt to have an extra set of ears to listen out for danger."

"And it wouldn't hurt to have some extra firepower," she admitted. "But it's a lot to ask."

"You didn't ask. I offered."

"So you did." Her lips curved in a smile that softened her features, making her look far more approachable than she had for most of the drive.

*Far more dangerous, too,* he reminded himself.

"I do appreciate the offer to stay, but—"

"But you're a deputy U.S. marshal with a big gun?" She patted her purse. "Glock 226."

"Nice." He bent a little closer to her, lowering his voice. "I have a sweet Colt 1991 .45 caliber with a rosewood stock, and if you quit trying to get rid of me, I might let you hold it."

A dangerous look glittered in her eyes. "You're trying to tempt me with an offer to handle your weapon?"

He nearly swallowed his tongue.

She smiled the smile of a woman who knew she'd scored a direct hit. "You can stay," she said almost regally. "We'll negotiate weapon-handling terms later."

*Will Nix's protection be enough to keep Dana safe?*
*Find out in award-winning author Paula Graves's*
*THE SECRET OF CHEROKEE COVE,*
*on sale March 2014 wherever*
*Harlequin® Intrigue® books are sold!*

HIEXP69746